Pitcairn's Father

A Tale of John Adams, 'Bounty' Mutineer

Lionel Pettrick

Copyright © 2019 Lionel Pettrick

Thank you for purchasing this book. This book remains the copyrighted property of the author and may not be redistributed to others for commercial or non-commercial purposes. If you enjoyed this book, please encourage others to purchase their own copy from their favourite authorised retailer. Thank you for your support.

Formatting and cover design by Caligraphics
https://www.caligraphics.net/index.php

Contents

Chapter 1 - Pitcairn 1
Chapter 2 - Hackney 4
Chapter 3 - London 9
Chapter 4 - Morgan 19
Chapter 5 - Murder! 25
Chapter 6 - The 'Penelope' 31
Chapter 7 - The 'Bounty' 40
Chapter 8 - Cape Horn and the Southern Ocean 51
Chapter 9 - Otaheite 60
Chapter 10 - Farewell to Otaheite 72
Chapter 11 - Mutiny! 76
Chapter 12 - Tubuai 84
Chapter 13 - Voyage to Pitcairn 96
Chapter 14 - The end of the 'Bounty' 103
Chapter 15 - Pitcairn in turmoil 109
Chapter 16 - Sole survivor 120
Chapter 17 - Discovered at last! 128
Chapter 18 - Rediscovered 133
Chapter 19 - The world comes to Pitcairn 138
Chapter 20 - Paradise? 142
Epilogue 145
Author's note 146
About the Author 149

Chapter 1 – Pitcairn

This side of the grave, silence does not exist. It did not exist in London, or on any ship I have known. Here, even when the wind is still and the birds are at rest, there is always the sound of the sea. Wherever I face, it is in my ears, in my every waking feeling, and maybe in my sleep, too. I have set foot aboard but two sailing vessels since I came to this place nearly forty years ago, and Pitcairn is so distant from other lands, and so small, that I often feel I have been sailing all that time. I once heard tell an old legend about a sea captain, a Dutchman I think he was, condemned to sail the oceans for ever. I do not recall why he suffered that fate, or know if the wickedness of mariners condemns them to an eternity on or under the waves, but if God's punishment was to leave me on this spot in the ocean, I have become content to accept His will. Once, when the Navy found this place again I feared I would be making another voyage, to London to be hanged, but the Good Lord softened the heart of Sir Thomas, Captain Staines, who saw that I had wrought peace and godliness here, and he allowed me to stay.

Long before that, before we came here, the King's Navy had named this island Pitcairn. Thus it was shown on their chart, and I never heard it had any other name. Myself, I've had other names. Since I came to this place I have taken back the name of my birth, John Adams, but I sailed under Captain Bligh as Alexander Smith. The people here love me, and call me Father. That is a name I can take pride in, as those others are sullied with wickedness and disgrace.

I am past sixty years of age, and I feel the strength departing my body. I am hindered by corpulence, and can no longer ascend the steepness of this island without feeling my heart pounding in my breast while I labour for breath and my head becomes light. But I have lived far longer than all the men who came here with me on the 'Bounty'. Ned was the last of them and it's nearly thirty years since the Lord took him. The others could not fight off the Devil, and their lives were destroyed. But Ned – Edward Young was his name – was a good man, not like the others. He told me that he was born in the West Indies, but his family was poor, not like most of the white men there who had great plantations and hundreds of slaves to do their bidding. So he came away to sea, and finally it was the two of us who changed this island from a Hell into a peaceful place. He had some schooling as a boy, which I never did, and he would read the Bible with me. He taught me a little of reading and writing, so that I could read the Bible and unite our people in prayers even after he was taken.

But I am no scholar, and I can not write these thoughts as they come to me. I am telling them to John Buffet. I was grateful when he, a carpenter by trade, and his friend John Evans joined us and took up burdens which I carried alone for many years. I now have hope that these new people can help our community to grow after I am gone. It matters not how humble or exalted the origins of our people, Pitcairn gives all who come or are born here the opportunity to cast off their sin and degradation and live in piety and harmony.

The cry of seabirds has been in my ears since my childhood. There they roosted and foraged in the marshes. Here the cliffs and high crags which form a fortress, and sometimes I think a prison for us few mortals, are the haven for so many thousands of them. Yet there is another cry which daily gladdens my ageing heart, the shouts and laughter of our children as they play, and the chanting as they learn their lessons or say their prayers.

I can not help but wonder what I might have become had I been raised in benign surroundings such as these, in love and security and a sufficiency of the necessities to keep body and soul together, available to all who have the will to delve the earth, to husband our livestock and to fish in the sea. Here there is no landlord or tax collector to be paid, and no poorhouse awaiting those who can not satisfy those ravening claws. Here we are poor, but gold and silks and fine mansions would avail us naught even if we had such things.

Chapter 2 – Hackney

I remember almost nothing of my life before the poorhouse in Hackney, a village outside the City of London near some marshy lands and a river which flows into the Thames. The house was not large and I think there were never more than thirty men and women there along with some of us children. I had two older sisters and a brother seven years younger than me, named Jonathan. We were left as orphans not long after Jonathan's birth, from which my mother never recovered. My father had already been taken some months before, drowned in the Thames. He worked for a merchant, ferrying goods from ships in the river, but the lighter he was sculling overturned because someone had loaded it badly – or so my poor mother told us midst her tears.

My father was also named John Adams, and came from Ireland. Without him to support us we moved to the poorhouse, and not long after, my mother went to The Lord as well. My two sisters were already grown women and moved away from the place, leaving me and my baby brother to the mercies of the poorhouse. Mr Woodlea, the Superintendent of the house seemed to resent our presence, I know not why, probably it was a dislike of children, but he never had a kind word to say to me, and I was in constant fear of his harsh tongue. Even now, sometimes in my dreams I see his ruddy face with giant spectacles resting on a purplish nose, and his booming voice uttering curses at the merest provocation. A woman called Martha suckled my little brother and was kind to me. For a while I stayed in the women's room and they shared their victuals with me as Mr Woodlea made scant allowance for myself. I helped them in their daily tasks, cleaning the house, spinning rough yarn and preparing the food. Once in the kitchen I was spied by Mr Woodlea taking and eating a small morsel of cheese that had dropped on the floor. He went into a fury, seizing a dog whip and giving me several lashes. That was the first time he beat me. Now I hated as well as feared him.

After a few weeks I was taken away from the women and placed in the men's room. As the house was not large I still saw Martha sometimes during the day, but the men were forbidden conversation with the women, and if Mr Woodlea saw me talking to her he would beat me. I think his resentment of me grew at this time because the men would not accept, as the women had done, that they should share their portions with me. As one, the men applied to Mr Woodlea and prevailed on him that their rations were scarce enough to fuel their own bodies for the hard labour they were given, and that he should make an extra provision for me. The Superintendent relented but only grudgingly, as he said that a child should not need a man's portion when he could not do a man's work. So my rations were mostly scraps, less than half the men's allowance, and I often went hungry. Soon I came to feel that thieving to satisfy hunger is not a sin, and I took any opportunity that came my way to steal from the kitchen. Sometimes I was caught and beaten, but the chastisement now served only to increase my determination and cunning.

The men were given work in the parish making roads and digging ditches to drain the marshes, and I was sent along with them to do what I could. The poorhouse was also given other tasks such as picking oakum, which I hated. The fingers of a child are ill-suited to clawing hardened tar from old hemp rope, and mine were made sore and bloody, but if I failed to produce a pound and a half of clean hemp in a day I was given no dinner. On Sundays we did no work, but would attend St John's Parish Church, sitting in the hindmost pews, the men to the right and the women to the left. As the gentlefolk of the parish glanced at us with pity and scorn, I wondered how much the gold watch-chain stretched across that gentleman's ample stomach would fetch, or how many coins nestled in his lady's purse, enough I vow to afford a whole roast chicken.

Thus I lived in that gloomy house for about a year, until I fell sick. One morning I was stricken by a strange fever and fell down in the road where we were working. They laid me on a bank till the end of the day, then I was carried back to my house and put in my cot. The fever became worse and I vomited back the little broth I was given. Then the rash appeared, and when Mr Woodlea saw it he fell into a rage.

"Hell's teeth ," he roared, "'tis the smallpox, I vow! Have him out of the house this instant, or he'll be the death of us all! You two," he snarled at the nearest, "sling him in a blanket and take him away."

"Take him whither?" asked one of them.

"Show him in the village, and see who will care for him there. Or you may throw him in the marsh for aught I care."

In the village they put me down by the parsonage, and called for the parson to come out. He cast me a glance and said, "Poor boy. He may not be long for this world, but you had best take him to the hospital at Moorfields. His father worked on the Thames, did he not? They look out for seamen and their families, so be sure to tell them that his father was a seaman."

Thus those two honest men did not throw me in the marsh, but plodded with me all the way to Moorfields. An attendant with a kindly face but sad eyes, whose name I do not remember, asked me

"What is your name, boy?"

"John Adams, sir," I croaked, for my mouth and throat were sore.

"How old are you, and where are your family?"

"I am eight years old, I think, sir. My parents are dead, my elder sisters have gone away and I have a baby brother at the poorhouse in Hackney, where I was living. My father was a seaman sir, he drowned in the Thames."

"Ah," said the attendant, "well, we will do what we can for you. In four weeks you will either be mending or you will have met your father in the next life."

The hospital was made up of several houses, and they put me in one away from the rest, where there were several sufferers from the smallpox, as well as other infectious diseases, particularly one which I have since seen many to suffer from, as it is common amongst sailors, known as the venereals. In that place I lay while my body fought the fever and the torment of the boils. Sometimes they applied some ointment where the boils raged, and daily gave me broth as well as some foul-tasting potions, I know not what they were. Finally I felt my strength to come back by degrees, and the scabs from the boils started to fall away, leaving the scars on my face and body which you see today.

Soon I was strong enough to walk outside, away from the foul smells and sights of the poor unfortunates who remained, many of whom would never leave alive. Then the attendant with the sad eyes said to me,

"John Adams, The Lord has spared you for some other purpose. We can keep you here no longer, and your bed is needed for others. Farewell."

I walked through the lanes to Hackney, with the sun on my face and birdsong in my ears, my heart uplifted. How soon was it cast down again! I knocked on the poorhouse door, which was answered by Woodlea himself. He obviously had not expected to see me again, and the look of surprise on his face quickly turned to rage and disgust.

"Why, you pox-ridden mongrel," he sneered, "what brings you here?"

"I am well again, sir, and I wish to take my place again here."

"Well again, is it?" he boomed. "You look like a bundle of disease, and there is no place for you here."

"But I have no other place to go to," I cried, "and my little brother is here, is he not?"

"I shall not answer to you for your brother or anything else. You brought disease to this house, and you shall never enter it again. Begone!"

Then he slammed the door in my face.

Chapter 3 – London

Now I was truly alone in the world. My baby brother was in the house, but I could not go to him, and if I could, there was little I could do for him. I could only hope that Martha would care for him and that God would somehow bring us together in the future. I reasoned I would get scarce charity in the village, and they would only direct me back to the poorhouse. So, like many lost souls before me, and I'll warrant since, I decided to seek my fate in London.

The smell of the City comes to you before you come to the City. Indeed, many times when the wind was westerly, a strange odour could be smelled in Hackney. Now as I reached the outer confines of London I could see whence it came as it over-powered my nostrils. Rain was by now falling and the foul mud in the streets and passage-ways mingled with the smell of wet horses and their droppings. There were few fine buildings, the streets were crowded in by hovels and shacks. Suddenly I heard a shout, " 'Ware below!", and as I looked up a hand holding a chamber-pot shot out of a window and tipped the contents in front of me. A little way along, a butcher threw some rotten scraps from his stall into the ooze, whither some yelping dogs eagerly descended. In regarding this disgusting spectacle I stumbled over something in the mud and saw that it was a dead cat.

By now I was tired and hungry, for I had covered many miles since leaving Moorfields that morning. I tried to beg a copper from a man in a fine-looking coat, and another who followed him, but they cast me not a glance and hurried past. Then I came to a shoe-mender's shop, where a man stood at the door. I asked him for sustenance.

"Who are you, and how come ye here?" he asked. I told him. "And were ye ever up before the magistrates, or pursued for any offence?"

"Nay, sir, never."

"Very well, I'll trust 'ee. You watch my door for me, and mind no-one takes my tools or my last. I go to that tavern over there a while. When I come back I'll bring 'ee vittles."

He walked to a tavern across the street, and I sat down in the doorway, grateful for the rest and shelter. It might have been two hours before he came back, and he was clearly drunk, but he was as good as his word for he bore a mug of beer and some bread and cheese, which I fell upon like a beast of prey.

"Now be off," he said, "but if you come by again you may be of some service to me. No promises, mind."

I took to the darkening streets and wondered where I may lay my head. Some houses I passed were little more than ruins and appeared to have no regular dwellers there, so I ventured through the half-open door of one and looked into the gloom. I saw no other person there, only rats scuttling away and the fluttering of pigeons. I found a dry corner and settled down for the night. I was cold, but fatigue overcame me and no-one disturbed my slumber.

In the next days I wandered the streets of that noisome city, with no clear idea of how I might improve my lot. Strangers mostly rebuffed my pleas, though a few gave me a farthing or two for holding their horse, or similar tasks. Some house-maids or shopkeepers spared me a crust of bread or a scoop of broth, but too often I retired in hunger to the dirty hovel where I shivered through the night. Increasingly I turned to the cobbler who had first shown me charity, Franklin was his name. As before, he would leave me to mind his door while he passed an hour or two in the tavern. I know not how he made sufficient for himself either, as few sought his services while I was there.

I was seated at his door one day when I heard a commotion and a boy came running from round a corner. As he passed me, with a deft movement his hand dropped something into my lap. I reached down for it, just as a large gentleman came bowling past, panting with his exertions and purple with rage, shouting "Stop thief! Where is the little devil!" He trumpeted his anger, which could be heard long after he disappeared from my sight.

In my hand was a watch and chain, like those that adorned the gentry in those Sunday congregations in Hackney. I felt excited, yet fearful and confused. What should I do with it? Its owner was long gone, but even if I found him he might accuse me of the theft, or in some other wise dissipate his anger on me. If I sought to dispose of it I would be hard put to explain how I came by it, and as yet I knew little of the ways of this city, or whom I could trust. I resolved to keep my own counsel for the time being, and concealed the watch in my rags. Presently Franklin came back, and I devoured the small portion that he brought me, saying nothing of what had occurred, and then left his shop.

I had gone but a few paces down the street when a voice behind me whispered,

"Say, cully, do you still have it?"

I turned round and was confronted by the boy who had run past the door earlier. He was a little taller than I, maybe a year or two older, with fair hair, lean and in rags like myself.

"Do I still have what?" I replied.

"Why, the watch," he replied. "I dropped it in your lap as I ran by. I was afeared someone might lay hands on me if the gull caught up, and if they did 'twere better they had no proof it was me that took it."

"So you stole it?" I said.

"Why of course, else how can poor boys like us keep body and soul together? Do you not know that London is a den of thieves, some wear fine clothes and jewellery and gold watches, and many more are just like us. So let me have it back."

Maybe along with the soot and miasma of filth of this city I had already imbibed some of its low cunning.

"But as you passed it to me, and it was not yours, is it not now more mine than yours?" I said.

"You wish to fight for it?" he scowled. "I have friends, you could not last long against us. Look, cully," he said, "I can see you know little of things, so I'll not be hard on you. Let me introduce myself. I'm Dick, who are you and where are you from?"

I told him my story.

"Well, Jack, here's the way of it. Now you have the watch, so let's say it's yours. You can't eat it, and if you try and sell it in the wrong place you'll end up before the Magistrate and get a whipping at the very least. I know who will give us a good few shillings for it, so, let's say we're partners and we'll take an equal share. What say you?"

I nodded and shook the hand he held out to me. Then he turned and I followed him through a maze of streets and alleyways deeper into the city, till we came to a gloomy street where the buildings closed in on both sides and the sunlight seemed shut out. Along the street stood many stalls, all heaped up with old clothes, and porters with more such bundles stumbled through the mud.

"This is Rag Fair," said Dick. "Most of them are Jews, but I know one who has a trade in more than old shirts and pantaloons." He ducked into a shop doorway, calling out "Ephraim!" as I followed him. In the dim room an elderly man with reddish hair below a skullcap, and spectacles on his long nose shuffled from behind a pile of drab coats and grunted a greeting.

"This is Jack, a new friend," said Dick, "he has something for 'ee."

"Something, eh?" muttered Ephraim, casting me a glance of malevolent suspicion. "And might that something be a whistle to summon the Bow Street Runners?"

"Nay, I'll vouch for him. Come on, Jack, show him the watch."

I handed it over, and the old man went to a drawer where he took up an eyepiece and examined it, muttering and grunting all the while. Finally he said, "It's a fair piece, good gold, I could give you ten shillings for it."

"Ten shillings!" protested Dick. I said nothing, feeling only delight at the thought of five shillings in my hand, far more than I had ever had before.

"Take it or leave it," Ephraim grunted, and made to hand me back the watch. But we took the money, and went out among the rag stalls. At one I purchased a coat for a few coppers. It was old and stained, rather too large for me and smelled a little, but now I felt more able to face the cold nights. Then Dick took me to a tavern where we feasted on mutton and fresh bread and cheese, so that, with my belly filled as almost never before, I felt drowsy.

"Now," said Dick, "you shall come with me and I will show you more of how the likes of us can live in this city." He led me through several alleyways to a low building which had few windows, and these were all blocked up. By the dim light of one candle I could see several boys, some the size of Dick and me, others maybe older. The room was little cleaner than the hovel where I had stayed before. But it was warm.

"This backs onto a smithy," explained Dick, "and the furnaces are close to that wall. Nobody bothers us here. These fellows all live by the speed of their wits and their fingers, and their fleetness of foot. If you wish to learn the trade we can work together a while as partners." The warmth of the room and my full belly persuaded me readily to assent to his proposition, then I lay down in an empty space and was soon asleep.

Thus I embarked on a career as a thief and a pickpocket.

I soon became an accepted accomplice of the ragged band who made that place their home, and progressed in my apprenticeship though my masters were little older than myself. The teeming streets and markets of London were our factory floor, and the unwary, the drunks, or the innocent visitors from the country were the stuff from which we spun our yarn. An older boy named Ben worked as a team with Dick, and they took me with them. They would bid me follow nearby while they wove their way through crowds, often passing each side of their victim, one catching his attention while the other extracted the contents of his pockets. The booty they would pass to me so that the evidence of their crime was no longer there if they were accused.

At the end of the day we repaired to our lair to examine our haul, which might be a few pence or shillings bound up in handkerchiefs, or purses with similar, silk handkerchiefs, and trinkets such as a silver thimble or clasp, as well as other small pieces stolen from market stalls, all of which yielded a few more shillings from Ephraim's coffers. My share from this was a shilling or two, not riches, but enough to ensure I never went hungry as I feasted on boiled beef and pudding, or at least broth and a loaf of bread. On a visit to the Rag Fair I also spent a little on a shirt and breeches, and a pair of shoes, none perhaps fit any longer for a gentleman, but all a great improvement on the rags in which I had come to London.

This was my life for above two years, in fact nearly three, and thieving no longer seemed a sin as I now had no thought of earning a living any other way. Now I had acquired the light-fingered skills of Ben and Dick and the others, and could hoist a purse from a pocket or a trinket from a stall with the best of them. But even the best sometimes get caught, and one day it was my turn. I was loitering outside a tavern on the lookout for gulls who had quaffed too liberally and were not in full command of their wits when I espied one who appeared to be a likely mark. He was a portly man, his attire in some disarray, and I had a glimpse of a pocket-book inside his overcoat. I approached him from behind, but as my hand touched on my quarry someone called out to him and he turned and seized my arm.

"Why, you young vermin," he roared, "I'll have none of this! Call out the constable!"

He held me in an iron grip and boxed my ears until the constable came and led me away to Bridewell, where I was cast in a noisome cell already full of men and boys of all ages. The following morning, hungry, thirsty and frightened, I was taken with the others to a pen at the court to await my turn before the Magistrate.

"Mercy, 'tis the Blind Beak himself today!" exclaimed one of those beside me.

"Who is the Blind Beak?" I asked.

"That is Sir John Fielding, the Chief Magistrate. He can be very harsh if you have been before him previously, but on a lad of your age he may go easy if it is your first time."

Some hours passed as I watched the others being taken up to their trial. Finally I was thrust into the dock, while my accuser, the man I attempted to rob, recounted the incident of the previous day. His name was Pountney, a merchant of some standing in the City, and the Magistrate showed great deference towards him. Then he turned to me;

"Your name, boy!"

"John Adams, sir." In my terror it had not occurred to me to try to conceal my true name.

"Where are your parents, how come you here?"

"My parents are dead, sir, and I was cast out of the poorhouse at Hackney after I caught the smallpox."

Lionel Pettrick

"Well, John Adams, it is my duty to keep the streets free of miscreants such as you, so that upright citizens such as Mr Pountney" - he inclined his head gravely towards my accuser - "can go about their business in safety. Though it is but your first offence, I will teach you a short lesson, you shall be whipped. But if you come before this Court again, you must expect a much severer punishment. Take him down!"

The whipping was little harsher than that which I had sometimes suffered at the hands of Mr Woodlea, but it seemed to me that the Blind Beak's regard for Mr Pountney had caused me these stripes, whereas I would have escaped with a warning, had my accuser been a lesser person.

I resolved for a time to be more cautious and seek another trade. I still slept of a night at the hovel by the smithy, although it became evident that the others tolerated my presence but grudgingly, now that I rarely took part in their daily exploits. I wandered the streets in search of employment, and increasingly stopped at the banks of the Thames watching the fishermen coming and going in the small craft they called peterboats. There I could glean a copper or two helping them sort their catch or carry it to a stall for sale, and I learned to mend a net and splice a rope. These boats appeared frail against the ebb and flood of that great river, and for a time my sleeping and rising were governed, as were the fishermen, by the tides.

Content would I have been with this way of life but for my return to the poverty of my younger days, and I could no longer afford the ample dinners taken by my dormitory companions, or replacements for the clothes on my back which were turning to rags. Ben and Dick could see my impoverishment and were forever urging me, sometimes kindly, at other times mockingly, to rejoin them in their enterprises. Thus was I led again into temptation and to a fateful day.

It was a stormy day as I ventured out into the lanes with Dick, and the wind was whipping at the coat-tails and plucking the hats of the heads of the unwary. I even saw the wig fly off one gentleman's head, causing much laughter amongst his companions as they made sure to hang on to theirs.

"I know a silversmith who neglects to keep his wares safe," said Dick. "Do you wait outside and keep a lookout for the Watch. I'll pluck a pretty piece and pass it to you as I leave, and when Ephraim has given us a few shillings for it we shall dine well this evening."

We came to a shop doorway and he peered cautiously into the gloom before entering, while I scanned the street, which seemed less busy than normal, I suppose because of the wild weather. It was but a few seconds later when I heard a shout of rage, and Dick came rushing out of the door, thrust something into my hands, and made off down the street, swift as a pigeon before the wind. The shopkeeper burst forth shouting "Stop thief! Call out the constable!" pointing at Dick's fleeing figure. I walked away slowly in the other direction, as was our normal way of completing such robberies. In my hands was some sort of silver goblet, which I made to conceal under my coat as I walked. But the wind caught my coat so that the object was not hidden as quickly as it should. A woman saw this and shrieked "He has it – that boy, seize him!"

So now I had to run, this time maybe for my life. If I was taken before the Magistrate again, would I hang this time? At the very least I could expect a severe flogging, not a little whipping with a birch. Or might I be transported to penal servitude in some distant colony? Such were my thoughts as I fled through alleyways before cries of "Stop thief!" as I prayed that in my haste I might not turn into one whence there was no issue.

Most of my pursuers lacked the youth and vigour to follow me far. But there was one man, younger than the rest and as fleet of foot as I, so that he was gaining on me and might finally overtake me. And then I tripped and fell in the mud, and the silver cup flew from my grasp. Now it must be all up with me, but at that moment there was a mighty gust of wind, and I heard a cracking, breaking sound. I had just passed a pawnbroker's shop, and as I watched from the ground I saw that the large metal sign hanging on the frontage was caused to be torn from the building by the force of the wind, taking much of the plaster and timber-work with it. The metal balls of the sign were heavy, and one of them fell directly on the head of my pursuer, so that he fell senseless to the pavement.

In the confusion that followed nobody took any notice of me. People came out from the neighbouring shops and houses to see what had happened, and gathered round the collapsed shop-front, and the body on the ground. A woman bent down to look more closely.

"He's dead!" she cried, "the poor soul!"

I slunk away like a muddy rat. I was afraid to seek out the silver cup lest I draw attention to myself, and I saw someone pick it up and gaze wonderingly at it, then showing it to his neighbour. Back at the hovel there was some ribaldry when the others heard how I escaped capture. Dick mournfully agreed that my loss of his booty could not be helped, but some others scorned me for failing to retrieve the cup, and I knew I could no longer stay in this den of thieves. I could not help but feel then, as I still do, that there was a man who might still be walking this Earth had it not been for my wickedness. May God forgive me.

Chapter 4 - Morgan

Casting around for a better way to continue my life, my feet seemed inevitably to carry me where I had been before, to the Thames and the fishing folk thereon. I made myself useful where I could, sometimes without reward but more often I was given a few halfpence or some broth or scraps for my labour. Thus I kept body and soul together, and it was not often that I passed a day entirely without sustenance, but at night I often longed for the warmth of the thieves' dormitory, as I could find nowhere as comfortable. The places where I sought shelter offered little protection from the elements, or from the rats which sometimes awoke me as they ran over my face and body.

After some weeks, however, my fortunes improved. One morning I was hailed by one of the fishermen, Morgan was his name.

"Hey, lad, come over to me!"

He was an old man, his hair and beard were white, his face tanned and cracked like old leather, and his eyes watery. He looked me up and down, but not in a hostile or lofty way like those in the public gallery of court or the Hackney Church congregation.

"What brings you here every day?"

"The same as you, sir, I would think. I need to earn my daily bread."

He laughed and said, "So you have learned no trade? Have you been fishing or on the water before?"

"No sir, I had no regular employment, only the likes of what you seen me do here." I thought better than to mention the apprenticeship which I had recently abandoned.

"Well, I've seen thee at ropes and nets, maybe you are ready to become a fisherman. Here," he brandished a rope frayed at the end, "put a back-splice on that for me."

Fingers already hardened by picking oakum could easily entwine the hemp strands, and Morgan's fellow fishermen had shown me the way of it some weeks before. I handed the rope back to him.

"It's well enough," he grunted. "What's your name, lad?"

"John Adams, I come from Hackney."

"Well, John Adams from Hackney, as you see, I am an old man and will soon become too feeble to work on this river. If you will work with me I can make you a fisherman, and you shall have a share of the catch. That may be little at first, but can increase as you do more and I do less. How say you?"

I readily agreed, and that same morning we set out on the tide together, as we did many mornings thereafter, and I felt more contentment in that period than ever I did until I came to Otaheite and Pitcairn. I was together with Morgan more than three years, and he became as close as a father, as by then my few memories of my real father were fast fading.

My life with Morgan followed a more tranquil path than with Dick and the others, and away from the bustle of the city we plied our small craft up and down some lower reaches of the river, and sundry creeks that flowed into it. Morgan showed me where we could drift with the current with a gill-net catching smelt and sprats, or the places where he set traps for eels, and cast out lines to get flounders and the like. The days were long, indeed we sometimes rose in the night to catch the ebbing tide and did not return till after night had fallen again.

Morgan was a man of few words, but sometimes he would tell a little of his past life. He had been many years a seaman, and as we passed great ships which towered over our little boat he could tell the history of many of them and whence they came or whither they were bound, the East Indiamen carrying all manner of goods, the colliers and the grain ships from our own coasts, and many vessels from the Low Countries, from Spain and Portugal and divers other places.

The catches we made earned a few shillings daily, and Morgan was as good as his word, giving me a portion of the takings, so that while I never felt wealthy, I was never afraid of going hungry to bed. Morgan had a room at a lodging-house and took me in with him, where there was a spare cot, so I could sleep in greater comfort than before. We worked every day when the weather was fair, even the Sabbath, and often in foul weather too. The winters were hard and very cold, with great slabs of ice sometimes passing us in the river. Morgan told me that a few years before the cold had been so great that the river up by London Bridge had frozen over so solid that it would bear the weight of a carriage and horses, and they had held a Frost Fair, which had been done in other years before that. There had been market stalls on the ice, and an ox roast and many sports and entertainments, and many folk came there. But I never saw anything like that.

Since I had left Hackney I had sometimes thought about my little brother Jonathan, wondering whether he was still alive. One day when the weather was too evil to venture out on the boat I thought I should go back to Hackney and enquire what had become of him. Thus, braving the rain and wind I found my way first to Moorfields, where I had been before, and thence to Hackney. With some trepidation, remembering the last time I was there, I knocked on the door and felt relief when it was opened by a woman.

"If you please, ma'am, I've come to find Jonathan Adams," I stuttered.

"He's at his lessons. What is your business with him?"

"He is my brother. I am John Adams, that lived here before, when he was a baby."

"Mercy me!" The woman bade me come in and shelter. I then learned that Mr Woodlea had died of apoplexy two years before, and his successor Mr Rogers, being a more kindly person, had decreed that the children should have a chance of improvement. There was now a school in the village and he had arranged for my brother and the few other poorhouse children to go learn to read and write.

She directed me to a house by the parsonage which had become the school, and there I waited a little while till the children ceased their lessons and came out. I called out "Jonathan Adams!" and a small boy turned towards me. I told him I was his brother, and we gazed at each other, hardly knowing what to say. We had but a short conversation before he was called back to his lessons. I let him know how I was situated, and he said he was happy and well cared for at the poorhouse, and would be pleased to see me again when I could come. Then I plodded through the rain and gales back to my berth at Morgan's lodgings.

During the rest of the time that I worked with Morgan, I took several opportunities when I was free to go and see my brother again. He was pleased to be told what little I could remember of our mother and father, and we discussed how we might be together in the future. I could not care for him at that time, and it was better that he should stay at the poorhouse and pursue what education they could give him. For myself, I could see no advantage in returning to the poorhouse, even if they would have me. And so the months passed, and I had little thought of any other life but that which I led on the river with Morgan.

Alas, when blind Fate casts temptation in our path, how easily does the Devil lead us to wickedness! There came another hard winter, when Morgan was often afflicted with a disease of the lungs, and his rheumy coughing made him weak and breathless. On many days he was unable to stir from his bed, but he had taught me well, and though still far from fully grown I had the strength and knowledge to work the boat and tend his nets and traps on my own, earning enough to keep the two of us from starving on the street.

One bitter day, however, the wind was blowing flurries of snow and whistling round the streets, so that Morgan, who was still unwell, counselled me not to go on the river that day. I went out in the hope of finding employment with the others, but there were few abroad, and they were of the same mind as Morgan. So, I gave up thoughts of work, and of walking to Hackney, too, in that bitter weather, and made for a tavern to take a little breakfast.

I arrived at the door at the same moment as another muffled figure, but as we both hesitated as to who should enter first, the other exclaimed,

"Why, young John! How goes it with you?" It was my old partner, Dick, much taller now, and much better dressed so that he could readily pass for a gentleman.

"Well enough," I said, "but by appearances not as well as you."

"So it seems," he replied, casting a glance over my drab apparel as I shivered in the piercing wind. He led me inside and invited me to join him at a sumptuous spread, of mutton, and game pie, and much more, far exceeding the fish broth which was my normal fare, and far more than I could afford. But Dick was generosity itself, and I was indeed glad to see him again, as these last years I had spent with Morgan were marked by honest toil and little excitement for a boy, and I had made few friends. I felt a little humbled as I told Dick how I had passed the time since we parted, as it seemed of little import in the face of his fine appearance and abundant purse.

"Well my friend," he said finally, "I see that you have chosen a hard life. I wish you well of it, but it would not do for me."

"A hard life, yes, but an honest one, I replied.

"Honest, is it?" he sneered. "Do you think the gentry will reward your honesty when you are coughing your life away in a garret like your master, or that the moneylenders will forbear to cast you in a debtor's prison when you can not pay them back because you were only unlucky, not dishonest? I choose to make a little wealth before I become honest."

Then he explained to me how he and Ben had advanced from dipping in the pockets of the unwary for a few shillings to robbery on the high roads into London, sometimes out to the west at places like Hounslow, or out beyond the turnpike on the Tottenham Court Road.

"The purses are much greater," he said, "and there's jewellery and other valuables to be had. From this last twelve-month I have a pretty penny stowed away. If I can make the same for another two or three years, I shall away to the country and marry and live like a gentleman."

"But maybe you will have an appointment with the hangman before then?" I said.

"Aye, there's the rub. And lately there's more danger than before. People have become more wary, and some of our escape routes across the fields are known to the constables, twice recently we have nearly been caught. We decided that we have to let that earth lie fallow awhile, which is why," he said, glancing at his watch, "I have come here today."

"How so?"

"We have another enterprise, but I should not tell you any more until I have spoken with Ben. You should go now, but come back at three o'clock and wait a half hour in the street, across from here. If I come, then maybe we have a use for you. If I do not, then I bid thee farewell, and you should forget that you saw me."

Chapter 5 – Murder!

I left him and went back to succour Morgan, who now seemed weak and very unwell. I procured some soup for him, and thought to fetch a doctor to tend to him, but there now remained to us only a few coppers, and little chance for me to earn more in the coming days without him. However, if I could join Dick's enterprise, just for once, I might secure the means to pay a doctor or an apothecary and to feed us until we could turn to our honest trade.

At three o'clock I returned to the appointed place, and Dick soon appeared, beckoning me to follow him. A few streets away he darted into the doorway of a lodging-house, and I entered behind him, mounting a stairway to a room which was evidently where he now stayed. Ben was already there. He greeted me coolly, and turned to Dick.

"Are you sure you can trust him?" he asked, "or will he betray us?"

"Nay, why should he," replied Dick to him, and to me he said, "Young Jack, you wouldn't give away your old friends, would you? We always stood by you, and we need to know that even if you part from us as you did before, you will never tell on us. We have a job which will pay well, and if you help us we will cut you in for a handsome share."

"I swear I will say nothing to anyone," I said, "and if I can quickly earn a few shillings I can hope to ease the suffering of an old man who has been kind to me these past few years."

"Aye, it should make you more than a few shillings," chuckled Ben, "so here's the way of it. We have come to know of a rich merchant who has a house in the City, but is lately gone away into the country, and most of the servants with him. There remain but one or two in the house which nevertheless has a rich trove of much value, gold and silver plate, jewellery and much coinage, and must be worth many thousands."

"But how come you know all this, and how can you enter without disturbing those who remain, and find what is worth taking?"

"We have fallen in with a servant recently dismissed from the household, so he bears a grudge. He says he secreted a key before he left the house, so we have an easy way in, and he will direct us to the right places inside. You can help us by keeping a lookout, and warn us if the Watch comes by. So, are you with us?"

There were to be many occasions later, particularly in the days following, that I wished I had bade Ben and Dick farewell and gone back to tend to Morgan as best I could. But I could not resist the lure of easy money, and assented without hesitation to join them. I was directed to the same place where I had lately met Dick, to be there at two o'clock in the morning.

Our meeting took place as planned, and we walked for fifteen or twenty minutes through the dark streets, successfully avoiding the Watch, or anyone who might wonder what we did there. Finally we came to a street where Dick pointed to one of the fine houses in the row.

"That is the one," he said, "When we go in, you should wait by the door and if anyone tries to come in, or looks as if he might disturb us, you can give a whistle. But where is our informant?"

Just then we heard some drunken singing, and espied a figure lurching along the pavement.

"Dear God, the fool is drunk!" exclaimed Dick. "We promised him a share, but to show good faith we gave him ten shillings, and he must have spent a fair part of it on gin. We can not take him near the house, he will betray us all. But does he have the key?"

We seized the fellow and came across the key in one of his pockets. Then we dragged him away from the street and into a lane where there was an entrance which led to a back yard with some stables. We cast him onto the midden and he lay there in a stupor. Then we cautiously approached the house, and reasoning that the key we had must be for one of the servants' doors at the side or back, we went round until we found a side door where the key turned in the lock.

I waited, shivering in the darkness, for it was another bitterly cold night, while the other two disappeared inside the unlit house. I had no way of telling how long it was, it may have been only fifteen minutes, but it seemed an eternity. Then I heard some shouting and singing, and I looked into the street where the reeling figure of our drunken informant was coming back, inevitably to betray us all. I ran back towards the door in the hope of warning my friends, but at that moment I saw an old man in a nightshirt holding a lantern come out, the caretaker I suppose.

"Why Enoch," he said, "what do you here? And who is this?"

The drunk made to lay hold of me, maybe in his befuddled mind thinking to exonerate himself by my capture. Without my two friends I could not overpower him alone, but then I saw, leaning against a wall, some sort of hoe or trenching tool that must have been left there by a gardener. I seized it at swung it at the drunk, striking him across the body, and he fell back into some bushes. But now the caretaker was upon me, and shouting at the top of his voice, "Robbery! Murder! Call out the Watch!"

I had to silence him, and I swung my weapon again, catching him on the side of the head. He went down, but he was still shrieking in agony, so I gave him another blow which clove into his skull and he shrieked no more. My companions had heard the commotion and came running from the house with bundles under their arms. I wanted to explain what had happened, but

Ben cut me short, hissing, "We must separate! Run for your life!" Then he and Dick made off into the night, and I fled in the opposite direction, taking a roundabout route through many quiet alleyways until I came back to our lodgings. In our room, Morgan was dead.

The dawn soon came, and I sought out the landlady of the lodgings to tell her that my friend and mentor was no more. She sent for the undertaker and made arrangements for the burial, and amongst Morgan's effects I found enough money to pay for that, but for little else. The landlady said that if I could not pay the rent I must quit the room. I was not minded to stay in any case, as I was anxious to find out whether there was a hue and cry for the robbers of that house, and if I might at least gain some reward for my part in it. I felt this was due as none of us might have escaped had I not silenced the old man so quickly. But I kept recalling the vile sound as my weapon cracked his skull, and I knew in my heart I must have killed him.

I set out to find Dick, and looked first in the tavern where we had met before but he was not there, and he was not to be found at his lodging. I knew not where else he might be found, so I stayed in the street near his house, hoping he would come back. Finally he did, after midday, and as he entered the door I called out to him across the street. He looked startled and afraid when he saw me, and made to shut the door on me, but then changed his mind and beckoned me to enter quickly. In his room he darted from corner to corner in great agitation, taking items from everywhere and thrusting them into a bag he had brought with him.

"Ben's been taken," he said. "We took some of the plate we stole to Ephraim, but he would have none of it, said it was a trade too dangerous for him. So Ben took it to another man, but he had already been warned by the constable to look out for this stuff, so he gave him up, and now he's in Newgate. And the old caretaker is dead. Ah, it was a bad night's work when you split his skull!"

"It was a bad night's work when you enlisted a drunken fool for an informant," I said, "and we might all have been taken had I not swung that hoe. But what of the drunk?"

"I fear he may be in Newgate as well, and they may accuse him of being the assailant. But here's the catch. Either of them might talk to save their necks and accept a lesser punishment. I hope Ben would not give me up easily, but he would not scruple to name you as the murderer, aye, and give your description too. The servant does not know you, and was so drunk he may not even remember you, but he has met me before, so I am not safe either. We must flee."

"But where shall we go?"

"Oh, we can not be together any more, you must look to yourself. I will go to the North or Scotland, you should go another way. Now go, and take this, there is no time to lose."

He put something in my hand and thrust me out of the door. In the street I saw that he had given me five sovereigns. So that was the price of a man's life. Now I felt more alone and terrified than ever in my whole life. I had no one to whom I could turn, I had scarce had the time to mourn for Morgan, and now I knew for sure that I, who never wished any man harm, was a murderer. I walked along streets without knowing where I was going, avoiding the glances of all passers-by and wrapping a cloth round my head as best I could, afraid that the pitted scars on my face might betray me. I dared not go back to the places where I was known, to the lodgings or the river and the peterboats, but some instinct told me that the Thames was my means of escape. Thus I found myself on the wharves at Billingsgate, busy with the commerce of many vessels large and small.

I was turning over in my mind whether it would be wise to escape by stowing away on some vessel, but I could not be certain of my reception when I was discovered, as for all I knew they might just throw me overboard, or bring me back into the arms of justice. But then I heard a fellow say to his companion as they passed, "There it is, the 'Penelope', where they are signing on."

I followed them to the gangway of a three-masted barque, a collier, to judge by the remnants of the cargo recently unloaded. At the gangway a man who I later discovered was the Captain inscribed the names of the two men before me. Then it was my turn.

"Name."

The name John Adams might now have been given to every constable in London. I remembered the name of a man who had stayed sometimes at our lodgings, a fat jolly man, a commercial traveller of some sort, I think.

"Alexander Gow."

"What experience have you, boy?"

"I've worked on the Thames above three years, sir."

"Hm, we'll give 'ee a chance, as we are short of hands at this time. We should sail in two hours with those that we have. Until you prove yourself your pay will be ten shillings a month."

In those two hours before the 'Penelope' slipped her moorings I offered many silent prayers that someone would not come and take me off to Newgate.

Chapter 6 – The 'Penelope'

After these many years on Pitcairn surveying the bright blues and emeralds of this Pacific sea, with warm breezes kissing my cheeks, I scarcely remember the stony grey of the North Sea, and the chill of the wind even on a bright day. But it was on the North Sea that I passed the next ten years or so, for the 'Penelope' was indeed a collier, plying between Newcastle and London, and sometimes to other ports in the south. In the river at Newcastle we discharged our ballast of sand, if we could into carts taking it to the glass factories, otherwise into the river, because above all the ship must be ready for its cargo of the black gold brought to us down the river by the keelmen on their launches.

The keelmen were very hard men, easy to quarrel with and much given to swearing foul oaths. They were very jealous in protection of their trade, and we the crew could not take part in the loading of the ship, which I did not mind. During those years, however, a new means of loading threatened the keelmen's trade, as the coal-owners built wharves where the ships could berth, and railways to them from the collieries, so that the coal came down in carts on the rails and was tipped into the hold down spouts. In London also, the crew took no part in unloading, as the job was reserved to men called "whippers". We took on the sand as ballast for the return voyage, and that was loaded by convicts.

So, over those long hard years I learned my trade as a seafarer, and the boy became a man. I was quick to learn the tasks of a common seaman, to climb the rigging, to set or reef sails, to take my turn at the wheel and to scrub the decks, although the Captain was less concerned about a clean deck and a polished binnacle than was Captain Bligh. After the first few voyages when the Captain saw that I could do my share, he increased my pay to fifteen shillings. There were many changes of crew, as some stayed only for a voyage or two, very few for more than three years, so that as I grew to manhood I also became a leading hand, and my pay had increased to twenty-five shillings a month. I think we sometimes lost crew to the Navy press-gangs, and I certainly did not wish to serve His Majesty at that time, as I was paid better than an Able Seaman.

Our crew was rarely above twenty hands, only half the number who sailed on the 'Bounty', and there were no officers. The Captain marked out those men whom he trusted, of which I was one, and left us to organise the watches. Captain Yates was past his middle years, a man of few words, but he saw to it that men did their work, and we were well fed and paid regularly, so that I was able after a time to add a few pounds to those sovereigns I still held, though I felt guilty every time I looked at them.

I took what opportunities I could when the ship was in the Tyne, taking on its load or bound by tide or weather, to go into the town, although it was a dark mean place, with children in rags, as I had once been myself, and many drunken men and women in the streets. I fear I fell prey to the blandishments of the whores who pursued us sailors, but I always felt disappointment at such dalliances, when in some dark corner the doxy would hitch up her skirts, and as we coupled I saw the wrinkles beneath the paint on her face, and her rotting teeth, and smelled the gin on her breath. But I had the urges of a young man, and could not forbear to try again when next I came ashore.

When we anchored in London I was for a long time very wary of going ashore, lest I might still be pursued for the crime we committed. But I think that the case was forgotten, because robbery and murder were such a daily part of life in London that the courts always had fresh meat, and earlier miscreants were unlucky or exceedingly stupid if they were later brought to book.

When I did venture out I took care never to visit the places where I had been before, or to make any enquiry about the outcome of that event. So I never knew if Ben was hanged, or whither Dick went, or any other matter concerning it.

I did, however, go to visit my brother whenever I could. He still stayed at the poorhouse in Hackney in the first years that I went to sea, but before I finished with the black gold trade he had found a position in the house of a merchant, and so was set on a better path in life than his brother.

The sea enters the blood of all those who learn to live with its moods, and I now thought of no other way of earning my living. I can not know how many more years I might have sailed on the 'Penelope', or if I would have gone in some other ship, or maybe been made a Captain. But I was not offered such a post when Captain Yates fell ill and retired, and another was appointed in his place.

The ship was owned by one of the colliery-owners, whom I never met, so I know not how our next Captain came to be appointed. He came on board in Newcastle, and spoke like a person of those parts, and, by God, he was one of the most unpleasant men I ever met. His name was Redepath, and he had a sly and evasive look about him. I heard him greet men with great affability, but when they were gone he would talk of them most despisingly, as I am sure he did about me when I was not there, and I always felt uncomfortable in his presence. I thought that if he knew anything to someone's detriment he would not hesitate to use it against them, and whenever he asked me questions about myself I was careful to tell him as little as possible.

With Redepath there came on board several rough fellows, as we were again short of crew. They seemed to me like the keelmen, but they worked the ship well enough as we sailed for London. We made several more voyages, but as the month wore on we found that our food was less generous than before, the bread was stale, and we once ran short of provisions when light winds caused us a longer passage than normal. It was clear that Redepath cared little for our welfare, and was never concerned to see that the ship was adequately provisioned. I asked the cook why, and he said that Redepath had given him little more than half the expenses that Captain Yates had provided. I confronted him about this and he said,

"Don't concern yourself, bonny lad, if we tighten our belts a little we'll all be eating the finest beef in a week or two."

He ignored my attempts to discover his meaning, and I felt great unease, thinking the time must come when I must find another berth. We came to London and discharged the coal, then loaded our ballast as normal, setting sail for Newcastle again, as we thought. But then some of the crew came to me complaining that, it being the month's end, we should have been paid. As a body we went to the Captain and asked for our wages. Then he summoned all the crew together, and addressed us as "shipmates", although I never felt such fellow feeling for him.

"Shipmates, I propose a little enterprise which can earn you double your normal wages. We go to take an extra little cargo which we can deliver before we go to Newcastle, and I have a customer waiting who will pay well. We sail south for France!"

So this was his ploy, we were to be smugglers! Along with some of the crew who had served under Captain Yates, I felt unhappy at this turn of events, but when I saw the men who had joined the ship with Redepath a few week before, laughing and cheering, I realised that they must have been privy to his scheme.

"And if we do not wish to proceed like this?" asked someone.

"Why, you are welcome to swim ashore," sneered Redepath.

This provoked more mockery from his "keelmen", as we were by now well into the estuary of the Thames, and not even the strongest of swimmers would make the shore through those treacherous waters. South we sailed, and across the English Channel into the Bay of the Seine, where we dropped anchor near a town which I think was Carentan. Redepath was rowed ashore and returned after a while with near a dozen barrels in the launch.

"This fine brandy is for the good burghers of England," he shouted, brandishing a pistol, "and I'll kill any man that touches a drop of it."

We set sail again for England, this time passing the Thames, and as night fell we entered an estuary a little further north, called the Crouch, where Redepath ordered us to anchor, and load the launch. He motioned me and three others into the launch and stepped in himself.

"There's an inn a mile upstream on the north shore called the 'Peterboat', he said. "They have a cellar at the water's edge where our cargo is awaited."

We rowed upstream in the darkness until Redepath ordered us in to the shore by the inn. There was no-one to meet us, which I saw made Redepath uneasy, but he told us to unload the barrels anyway. So he was a fool as well as a blackguard, because we must have been watched all the while, and no sooner was the last barrel ashore than there was a shout, "Stand, in the name of His Majesty!", and a shot, and one of our crew fell wounded into the boat.

"The Excise!" cursed Redepath, "we are betrayed. Quick get us off! Row for your lives!"

And row we did, and as we rowed I wondered how we had escaped so easily, as if the Excise-men had wanted to take us, they surely would have done so. But in the dark we did not know who our assailants were, and a pistol shot was sufficient to frighten us away, and leave our cargo behind without payment.

Returning to the ship, we turned as one upon Redepath, and demanded to know how he had led us into this folly. He was agitated and in some confusion, talking little sense, but when some of us again demanded our wages he confessed that the Frenchman from whom he had bought the brandy had demanded more than he expected, so he had used our money to supply the difference.

On hearing this there were shouts of rage, and one of the "keelmen" darted forward and felled him with a single blow. It was now clear that those who had joined the ship with Redepath were as much deceived by him as any of us. But now he lay lifeless on the deck, and we discovered his neck was broken. Though I had not landed the blow myself, I was glad that this sorry creature was no more. An untrustworthy man had treated us as fools, and then himself been fooled by both his supplier and his customer.

Now a furious argument broke out, as few of us could agree what we should do next. Some said we should sail for Newcastle and trust that the authorities would accept that they had desired no part in Redepath's enterprise, and were not all responsible for his death. But the "keelmen", particularly the man who had felled the Captain, spoke angrily against such a plan, reminded us that Redepath had cheated us all, we had not been paid, and no-one should have to face the hangman because of him. Then one said,

"We'll take the ship! We can find a place to scuttle it, then we're free of all this!"

"Aye, take the ship, but burning it will not make good our pay. If we sail for the Low Countries or France, we might sell it!"

"Or we take it away and join with the pirates!"

What was this madness! How should we destroy the ship and escape, or sail to other countries, or become pirates? Who could navigate away from familiar shores? I could see that some were ready to come to blows, and I wanted no part of this any longer. I spied the launch still alongside, as no-one had thought to hoist it aboard, so I quickly went down to my berth and collected the pouch with my savings, then ran back on deck and over the side, into the boat and away, before anyone noticed I was gone. In the dark I rowed across the river, away from the bank where we had landed before, hoping that I would meet with no more troubles that night. I came ashore in a muddy creek, and left the boat there, so that my clothes were covered in mud by the time I gained dry land. Dawn was breaking, and from its light I reasoned that I must have found the south bank, so that I might find a road towards London.

I came across a girl at a farm gate who gave me directions, and I set out for London, as I could not think where else to go. As I walked I felt relief at being off that ship, and away from those madmen, who must surely be courting disaster. But then it came to me that in seeking safety alone, I had maybe also set myself up to be named as Redepath's murderer, as it would be easy for the others to name me, and how could I swear my innocence against nearly twenty men who swore the contrary? So once again I must flee for my life, and avoid the places where I was known.

Nevertheless I continued the whole day towards London, as my greatest salvation lay in finding another ship there to take me away from England for a time. I passed not far from Hackney, and thought of my brother, and whether I should visit him, but I did not wish to lose time, and I was in doubt about what I should tell him of my present circumstances, so I decided to leave it for another day. I did not know then that I would never see him again. Now I recalled the Navy Dockyard at Deptford, and if I could find a ship there I would avoid London, so I turned my weary steps towards that part of the river in search of a ferry to go across. Darkness was falling as I came towards that great bend in the river, and saw the tall masts there, and found a ferryman who agreed to take me across for the price of his supper.

The air was chill, and I had not eaten since the previous day. I therefore repaired to a tavern, to slake my thirst and hunger, and ponder whether I might get away on a ship that very evening. As I sat with my tankard of ale, and bread and cheese, I could not help but hear the conversation of a group of men at the next table.

"The Captain comes aboard tomorrow," said one, "and we may expect to sail in the next day or two."

"But we have not a full crew," said another.

"That matters not," said the first speaker, "we sail first for Portsmouth, and we have enough hands to take her there. The Captain is anxious to leave, as there has already been so much delay because of the fitting out here. In Portsmouth we may easily be supplied by the press-gang if not by volunteers."

It seemed that Providence was already offering me my means of escape. I stood up and moved to the end of the table, awaiting a chance to join the conversation. The original speaker looked up.

"What, lad," he said, "if you're begging you'll get naught here."

"Not begging, sir," I replied, "but if you're short-handed I am in need of a berth."

"Indeed," he said, "and what is your name?"

I hesitated. Alex Gow should be no more.

"Smith," I said, "Alexander Smith."

He looked at my bedraggled figure. "Well, Alexander Smith, if that truly is your name, have you any experience of the sea apart from splashing in Thames mud?" His companions burst into laughter.

"Aye, sir, I worked around ten years on a collier plying between the North Country and London."

The party again laughed heartily at this revelation.

"Our ship was a collier, almost converted now to His Majesty's Service, so if what you say is true you may be better able to sail her than any of us. What was your ship? Have you papers?"

I thought quickly. It would be folly to mention the vessel which I had recently abandoned, but then I remembered another coal ship which had foundered with the loss of all hands some months before.

"T'was the 'Ebdon Maid', sir. It went down in a storm off Bridlington, and my papers with it. I was the only one to be saved."

"Very well, Smith. You may sail with us to Portsmouth. If you prove unfit you will be discharged there. If your work is good you can be retained as an Able Seaman, but you should know that our collier will make no mere coastal passages. After Portsmouth we may be gone from England for two years, so do not expect to see your wife or sweetheart again for a long time."

"I have no wife or sweetheart, sir, and I welcome the opportunity to serve His Majesty." I felt a pang that I would be missed by my brother, and I could not bid him farewell.

"Good. I am John Fryer, Sailing Master of His Majesty's Armed Vessel "Bounty". Report to me tomorrow on board at eight bells of the morning watch. But before then you should wash your rags or obtain some cleaner ones. The Captain pays much attention to cleanliness, and if he saw you as you are now he would not welcome you aboard."

"Thank you sir." For the first time that day I felt a calmness and a hope that I might finally leave the evil of my past behind, as I had hoped before, when I went fishing with Morgan, and when I had sailed with Captain Yates, so maybe this time the Navy would give me the simple honest life that I craved, for I never wanted to be a thief and a murderer, but had been led to commit such foul deeds by others. Straight away I went out and found a trader who furnished me with some old but clean clothing, after which I paid an ostler a few pence to bed down in the corner of a stable, where on sweet-smelling straw I fell into a deep and blessed sleep.

Chapter 7 – The 'Bounty'

Just after sunrise in the chill of early autumn I trod the wharves at Deptford's waterside in search of the 'Bounty'. There were several ships flying the Navy Ensign, but she was not among those alongside, and I enquired of a hand on the deck of one of them.

"The 'Bounty'," he laughed, "she's anchored off." He gestured at a vessel swinging in the slack tide. "You're going crabbing, then, or oyster fishing? They're loading her from the jetty down there."

I thanked him and walked down to the jetty where I stated my purpose and Mr Fryer's name, and then assisted with loading some stores onto the lighter, which ferried us to the ship. I well remember my first view of that ill-fated vessel. She did indeed resemble the 'Penelope' and those other bluff, sturdy ships which plied the North Sea coal trade. She was about the same length, but the masts were shorter than the 'Penelope', and she seemed to ride quite high in the water. I learned later that Captain Bligh had reduced the masts and ballast to ride the storms that he expected we would encounter. She resembled no warship, the reason I supposed for the man's reference to "going crabbing". I scaled the ladder and in the cockpit spied Mr Fryer in conversation with several others.

"Ah, Smith!" he said as I approached, "at least, I trust that is still your name this morning?"

"Alexander Smith is my name, sir" I replied with as much gravity as I could muster.

"Very well. These officers are Mr Christian, First Mate, Mr

Young, Midshipman, and the clerk, Mr Samuel. Go with him and enroll. Landsman's rate, Mr Samuel, as far as Portsmouth, and if he proves himself, an AB thereafter."

I went with Mr Samuels to his cabin where he inscribed my name in a ledger, then I stepped outside, where Mr Young was waiting. He was a swarthy slim-built man, in appearance the same age as myself, with an upright and friendly demeanour.

"Come, he said, "I'll show you to the fo'c'sle and you can scrap for your berth with the others." His accent was unfamiliar to me and I asked whence he came.

"From the West Indies," he said, "I was born in St. Kitts. My father was an Englishman, and made sure I had a good education, but his family disowned him and I had no desire to become a clerk to slave-owners, so I came away to sea some years ago. I fancy that we may be returning to the Caribbean this voyage. My friends call me Edward or Ned, though not in the Captain's hearing, unless you want a tongue-lashing or worse. And how came you here?"

I could not remember the last time I had been addressed at such length or with such friendship, and it shamed me to repeat the lie which I had uttered the previous evening.

"Ah well, I can see things have not been easy for you, you need say no more. Go find your berth."

I entered the gloom below decks and found a place to stow my meagre possessions, and sling a hammock. There were two men asleep in hammocks, otherwise the place was unoccupied. I stepped on deck again and reported to Mr Young, who directed me to join the gangs busy embarking stores and stowing them in the hold. I exchanged the briefest of greetings with those about me as I heaved bales and barrels. About an hour later we heard piping from above, and my neighbour said, "Captain's coming aboard." We paused briefly and the bark of command could be distinctly heard.

"I expect the pilot within the hour, Mr Fryer, then we weigh anchor immediately, we must catch this ebb to Long Reach. These damned shipwrights have delayed us long enough."

This was a bark with which we were all to become accustomed in the coming eighteen months.

"Why so much delay by the shipwrights?" I asked my neighbour.

"I know not why so long," he replied, "but they have been converting her from a coal-ship to a transport for plants. The whole Grand Cabin is given over to that, and the Captain roosts in a small cabin in the corner. We are to go gardening in the Tropics," he grinned.

The pilot duly arrived, and I was put to the capstan to weigh anchor. That afternoon the ship slipped quietly down the Thames and in the gloom of early evening we came alongside a jetty near Gravesend. During the next two days we loaded four cannon and twelve swivel-guns, with much ammunition and small arms, supervised by Mr Peckover, the Gunner, and Mr Coleman the Armourer, who did not escape the rough edge of the Captain's tongue for whatever reason.

"He wishes we were a ship of the line," muttered Mr Coleman, as we struggled to manhandle one of the heavy cannon into its cradle.

It was another three days before the wind and tide were favourable and we could escape the Thames into the open sea.

God knoweth all. It may be that, knowing the ship and many of its crew were doomed, He was giving us a sign of our fate by the difficulties we had in leaving England. Twenty days it took us to battle against adverse winds and stormy seas to come round the Kentish coast and along the Channel to our anchorage off Portsmouth. During this time the little community that is a ship's crew settled into its character – the friendships, the petty rivalries and jealousies emerged during that routine of watches, and you learned who was willing and dependable, and who was not. I mostly shared watches and messed with Jim Valentine, a young lad who had little to say for himself, also Will McCoy, John Millward and Matt Quintal, all hard men with years in His Majesty's service. Ned Young always spoke to us with respect and understanding, but of the other Midshipmen I found Peter Heywood to be distant, holding himself as a gentleman of superior rank and breeding, though he was no more than a boy, and in those first storms he became very sick, as he had never before served at sea. Among the officers I noticed a coolness between Mr Fryer and Mr Christian, as the latter seemed to consider himself superior by virtue of his friendship and previous service with Captain Bligh. He did indeed have the manners of a gentleman, as I believe he was one, and he was of an amiable disposition towards the crew, issuing orders without harshness.

It was rare, however, for the Captain to display much jollity. From those early days, his mood would change from tranquillity to angry rages. I had not expected to hear an officer and a gentleman utter oaths as foul as any keelman in Newcastle, but when Bligh perceived a failure of duty by those under him he did not restrain himself, although it was mostly on the officers that he vented his spleen. He was frustrated at the long delays in fitting out the ship, and now a voyage that in fair weather might take only a few days was holding him back from receiving his final orders in Portsmouth. It was also said that he was exceedingly displeased and disappointed with the Admiralty, as he had not been promoted from Lieutenant, as he expected when he accepted this command, so although on board he was addressed as Captain, that was not his rank.

Such matters, however, concerned me little as I took my place among my messmates, and showed Fryer and the other officers that Alexander Smith was a trusty seaman who could get aloft and take in a reef in the worst of weather, or turn his hand to any task as well as any man aboard. Mr Fryer was as good as his word, and when we anchored off Portsmouth he confirmed my enrolment as Able Seaman on full pay. Although we remained at anchor for two weeks there was little opportunity for a run ashore, but that concerned me little because upmost in my mind was the desire to leave my past life behind, and undiscovered. Little did I then know how completely that desire was to be satisfied.

The Captain, however, became fretful at the delay in receiving his orders, as the weather was fair for a passage westwards, and when he finally came aboard and gave the order to weigh anchor, the westerly storms which had plagued us before set in again. Although we made many attempts to beat down the Channel we were driven back time and again to anchorages off Portsmouth. The cold was severe, and got into the bones of Mr Fryer and Mr Peckover, who complained of the pain in their backs and all their limbs. Many others caught colds, and there was much coughing and sneezing. Maybe my years on the North Sea had hardened me against such ailments, as I did not become sick and was able to stand all my watches.

"Smith, you are a hardy fellow," Mr Christian remarked on one occasion.

"Aye, sir, the Channel is no worse than the North Sea," I replied, but declined to say more lest I revealed something I should not.

Our fruitless endeavours continued until just before Christmas Day that year, when the wind changed, and now it was a gale from the east that chased us down the Channel, and midst clouds and spray I caught my last ever glimpse of England. Some of us were ordered aloft to furl the main top-gallant, and one of the lads, Tom Ellison I think it was, lost hold and fell from the yard, but he grasped a stay and saved himself from breaking his neck or drowning.

The cook served us a fair Christmas dinner, and I think he did his best on that voyage although sometimes it was not easy to eke out the rations we had, for we were forty-six on board, officers and men, so far more than crewed a collier, and we were not able to have fresh provisions every week as I had been used to. I think Tom was his name, too, but he went on the boat with Captain Bligh after we took the ship, and I do not remember.

By Ushant, Nature's full fury was unleashed on us, and as we scudded under bare poles before the wind, huge seas crashed over the ship and broke loose the barrels and some of the spars as well as the boats on deck, and as we fought to secure them it was a mercy that none of us were washed away, but only some barrels went overboard. Another wave broke through the windows of the great cabin so that the ship took in a lot of water, and afterwards it was discovered that some of the bread and other stores were ruined.

Eventually the storm abated, and as we sailed southward into more pleasant weather we were able to dry our clothing, and our duties became more regular and more easy. Men now fell to wondering more about the voyage on which we were embarked. The Captain had made no announcement, but it was apparent that our course was not set for the West Indies, as I was first given to believe when I joined the ship. Mr Christian had remarked to James Valentine that we were to sail to islands in the Pacific to search for a plant which we would then carry to the West Indies.

There were two gardeners who had come one board with us, an older man, I remember not his name but he went on the boat with Captain Bligh, and his assistant William Brown, that came with us to Pitcairn and was killed – poor Billy! I fell into conversation with him one day, and he told me that he had been to sea as a midshipman before he took up 'botany', as he called it, and he must have been a seaman, as a landsman might nearly have died from sea-sickness in the few days before.

"What is 'botany', and why is the ship built as a nursery for plants?" I asked.

"Botany is the science and study of plants. The 'Bounty' goes in quest of a tree called Breadfruit, which grows in the Society Islands in the Pacific Ocean. We are to fill that cabin with young plants and sail with them to the West Indies where they may grow into trees. The fruits grow large and plentiful, and can be a wholesome food, like bread, for the negro slaves."

"Do not the negroes have food at present?" I wondered.

"Aye, plantains and cornmeal, I think, but if the breadfruit will grow as easily, as we think it should, in the West Indies as in the Pacific Islands, then the slaves may be fed more cheaply and plentifully."

Many times over the years have I recalled that conversation, and the look of despair, grief almost, on the face of Captain Bligh as the 'Bounty' sailed away from him and the others that went with him, and he was obliged to watch as Quintal and McCoy threw his precious breadfruit plants into the sea, jeering all the while. He felt this as a grievous loss, and as the voyage was commissioned by the Admiralty there was a loss to the common purse too, and some lost their lives, but the plantation owners, who were to benefit by feeding their slaves more cheaply, lost nothing. But at the time we spoke I knew nothing of that. I was simply pleased to have the sun on my back, and a fair wind taking me away from my troubles in England and towards new adventures.

After some days we came to an island they called Tenerife, and anchored there in a bay where there was a small town. The Captain sent Mr Christian ashore to find out from the Governor of the island whether we could be supplied with materials to repair the ship, and also victuals to replace those that were spoiled, and this was so. Young Jim Valentine was among the party that rowed Mr Christian, and told me that he had been into the town, and found ladies offering entertainment. The next day that Captain went ashore, and I was detailed to the boat-party, so I was much excited at the prospect of dalliance after a long time without such pleasure. But as we came there, the Captain ordered us all to remain with the boat and on no account to leave it, so I was greatly disappointed.

Then the next day the gardener wanted to go and look at the plants that grew on the island, and I rowed ashore with him also. This time there was no order to remain with the boat so we drew lots for one to remain on guard, and the rest of us went into the town. It was a poor place, as poor as the meaner streets of London, but as I hoped, I tumbled with a wench who was still quite young, though her breath smelled sour, not of gin but of wine.

Five or six days we were there, and then set sail towards the south. As the air became humid the Captain was much concerned, as he always was, with the cleanliness of the ship, so that we could air our bedding and clothing, and decks and bulkheads were cleaned and washed with vinegar, which we did many times during the voyage. In lighter airs I was also able to return to my old trade, as we trailed fishing lines and caught some dolphins.

There was a strange incident during those days, as while we aired our bedding the Captain also ordered the examination of some of the stores, and when the barrels of cheese were opened, it was found that two cheeses were missing from one of the barrels. The Captain became angry, and said they must have been stolen. He ordered that no cheese should be issued for the period in which the ship would have consumed as much as was missing, and there was much disquiet amongst the men, and the officers too, for no-one could account for the missing cheese. James Morrison, Boatswain's Mate, claimed that it was Bligh himself who had it taken out and sent to his house in Deptford before we sailed, but I can not see how Bligh would have made such a disturbance about it if that had been true. Maybe we were all the victims of some thievery at the dockyard, but we went short because of it, and never learned the truth.

There was one amongst us in that fo'c'sle who was disagreeable to us all, he was Michael Byrne, an Irish man I think, who could never count anyone as his friend, because he dealt only in insults and mockery. His duties were very limited, and he would never go aloft because he was near-blind, but the Captain took him on because he could play the fiddle very well, and the Captain valued the exercise of dancing as much as cleanliness. So in all but the foulest weather, at four o'clock in the afternoon we were obliged to dance to Byrne's fiddle, whether we wanted or no. At first we thought this amusing, and did not mind, but finally, day after day of jigging seemed as mighty tedious as the fiddler himself.

The Captain divided us into three watches, which was agreeable to all as we could sleep longer without disturbance, and he then appointed Mr Christian as Officer of the third watch. Later he announced that Mr Christian was appointed as Acting Lieutenant, and there was little doubt at that time that he looked on Mr Christian most favourably, and sought to assist his career.

At another muster of the crew Captain Bligh explained to us the object of the voyage, although we already knew most of it, that was, to sail to Otaheite in the Society Islands of the Pacific, and procure breadfruit plants to go to the West Indies. But he then said that his orders were to sail to Otaheite via Cape Horn, which was now our course, but because we had been delayed so long in setting out, the southern winter would not be far off when we approached those latitudes, so adverse winds and seas would make our passage into the Pacific Ocean extremely difficult.

"I have every confidence in my ship and in you, my officers and crew, that we can overcome any difficulties and dangers, and those who acquit themselves well will earn my gratitude and recommendations for promotion."

I think there were few on board who had made this passage before and could conceive of what we were about to experience, so we would have thought little of it, but he told us also that we must go on reduced rations because we might be a long time at sea before we could re-supply. We accepted the necessity, but our rations had already suffered because the beef we had been supplied at Tenerife was not fit to eat and most of it was thrown away. Byrne declared that it was not from a cow, but from a donkey, and someone said "only an Irish man can know that", which enraged him mightily. There were pumpkins which were starting to decay and we were served with them to eke out the bread, which all complained about, the officers more than us.

When we crossed the equatorial line they held the traditional ceremony, and I was among those who had not been there before, who had to pay tribute to King Neptune and suffer indignities for the amusement of others. I found no amusement in it, and I was glad I should only be required to watch it next time, but I could not know that I would never cross the line again.

Although the Captain was quick with his tongue he was slow with the lash, and it was not before we were well to the south and the weather was cold again that there occurred the first flogging on board. I heard raised voices one morning, and looked across to see Matt Quintal and Mr Fryer confronting each other angrily, and Matt had his fist raised, although he struck no blow. The cause of it I did not learn before the whole crew was called to muster and the Captain read the Articles of War, charging Matt with insolence and mutinous behaviour towards Mr Fryer.

Matt made no answer to the charge, and the Captain ordered twelve lashes, which were given by Morrison, who appeared to feel distaste at administering the punishment, as did Bligh for having ordered it, although he had no choice. Afterwards I went to Matt in his hammock and asked what had happened.

"When we tacked, Fryer cursed me and said I loosed the sheet before his command. I said I had as many years at sea as him and knew well enough how to tack a ship, and if he were such a fine officer he would not have been passed over for the promotion given to Mr Christian."

"Ah, Matt, you had as well stuck a knife in him as said that. You invited him to have you flogged."

"I know, but on every ship I've sailed I find the officers are fools and I never can forbear to show it, so I have been flogged many times."

Matt Quintal had a madness in him, so that it was not only the orders of officers that he could not accept, but the fellowship of any man, and he could not live in peace wherever he was, which was plain to all, long before he met his end at my hands.

Chapter 8 – Cape Horn, and the Southern Ocean

Now we drove hard to the south, towards the greatest test of a ship and men I would ever know. The wind became bitter, and sometimes the swirling snow and dim light of the sun gave the appearance that we were sailing into some ghostly Hades. Away to starboard we glimpsed tall forbidding peaks, which Ned Young said was a land called Tierra del Fuego.

"How could there be any life on there," I said, "with wind and cold like this?"

"Indeed," he replied, "I heard there are some poor savages live there, and scratch a living somehow. But I think they have no breadfruit."

We laughed, and then he told me that in days we would be abeam Cape Horn, the southernmost tip of the Americas, and beyond that were only the open seas and a frozen wasteland at the bottom of the world, so we must beat the ship west against the weather to arrive in the Pacific.

Nigh on a month we strove for that westward passage, but the Almighty would not grant it to us. Day after day the gales came out of a westerly quarter, and though we tacked with the wind-shifts time and again we could make little headway. Though the ship sailed well, and could have succeeded in calmer waters, the monstrous seas drove us back whence we had come. So many waves broke over the ship that it is a miracle that it did not sink, and I spent many hours at the pumps, where all hands took their turn.

The ship was sturdy and sound, but the overpowering weight of the waves that crashed down on her sprung leaks in planking and decks, so that no part was free from cold and damp. The Captain ordered fires to be lit below decks, and every watch to see to the drying of clothes. He also gave over the Great Cabin for some to sling their hammocks, and generally did what he could to ensure the comfort of all. But some became sick from the cold, and others were injured by the violent motion of the ship. We had a surgeon, Mr Huggan, who fell down and hurt a shoulder, but we all knew him for a drunkard, and Michael Byrne joked that he need not have come to Cape Horn, he could as easily have fallen in Portsmouth Harbour. Tom the Cook broke a rib, and another man hurt his back. Mr Peckover the Gunner again complained of rheumatism, and some men felt faint from exposure to the elements.

Yet in the midst of all we had some sport, though it had a serious purpose. We had caught few fish on our voyage, just occasional dolphin, porpoise or shark to supplement our diet, but now we caught seabirds. In our wake there always followed many albatross, and another bird they called pintada. We found we could catch them by trailing a line with some meat fixed on it a little way before the hook, so that when the bird went for the meat, a swift jerk on the line could impale the bird's body or feet on the hook.

The meat from these birds was meagre and fishy, but one of the gardeners suggested that we might improve them by keeping them in pens and feeding them corn – and it was so! In days they put on weight, and when they came to the table, those who had them fancied they were eating goose or duck, although I had known little of such fare before. We had brought sheep, poultry and hogs from England, but most of these had died or been consumed, so this other source of meat was welcome to us.

I wonder, if Captain Bligh had continued this battle against the elements whether we might still be there, because we kept the ship in good order, and never lost a spar or a yard of canvas. But after four weeks he came to the same mind as all of us below decks had been for more than half that time. He summoned all hands and shouted his thanks to us for attending to our duties during the last month.

"The season is against us and we can have no hope of more favourable winds and weather than we have had. We have all experienced the impossibility of beating round against these winds and waves, and I wish to lose no more time trying. I believe these same winds will give us a quick passage to the Cape of Good Hope, and thereafter to Otaheite eastward round New Holland. Bear away, Mr Fryer, and set a course for the Cape of Good Hope!"

We all gave three hearty cheers at that, though Jim Valentine muttered "And how soon before he has us back at the dancing-lessons?"

Four or five Sundays passed before we sighted that Cape, and the Sabbath was now observed without fail, which we could scarcely do in the previous month when the Almighty sent all the elements against us. The winds were still strong at times, but mostly from astern or nearly so, and as the ship surged down the waves we mustered on deck while the Captain said a prayer and read to us from the Bible, this Bible which I keep by me and try to read from every day, though it is still hard for me.

Aye, Jim, the Captain did order the dancing as we had to before, but we complained to the officers that we lacked the strength for this, as our rations were now small and of poor quality. Also, all were required to take their turn at working the pumps, which never ceased because the ship was leaking badly from the battering it had suffered. So Mr Christian persuaded the Captain that though he thought to make us healthy by the exercise of dancing, there was no benefit therefrom when men were weak from lack of good nourishment, and they were adequately exercised by straining on a pump handle. The Captain agreed, and Byrne fiddled only for his own amusement during the rest of this passage.

Lionel Pettrick

So it was that after four months at sea since leaving Tenerife we sighted the Cape of Good Hope and came round to Simon's Bay, as the anchorage by Cape Town was not sheltered from the gales that brought us there. But the relief we all felt was destroyed for one poor man, John Williams that was, a Guernsey man (who came with us to Pitcairn and was killed). He was heaving the lead as we looked for our anchorage, and called a mark too deep, I know not why, as this was a duty he had done before.

"God's teeth, man," Captain Bligh blazed in anger, "you'll have us aground, damn your eyes! I bring this ship to safety through seas that would defeat any captain, and you risk making us look fools in a harbour for all to see. Put him in irons!"

There were indeed several Dutch ships in the bay, and the Captain doubtless considered himself a better sailor than any of them, and such an injury to his pride was unthinkable. He went ashore directly, but the next day Williams was paraded before us and given six lashes, which he bore quite well.

We remained at this anchorage more than one month, a time of restoration for our bodies and for the ship. Now there were fresh provisions daily, meat, vegetables and bread, and we had some success fishing from the boats, both with nets and with lines. A party took a boat some leagues away, and came back with seals and seabirds which they killed on a rocky island. There was a bird like a goose which they said did not fly, they just knocked it over, but its flesh was not good to eat. In the meantime there was much work to make the ship seaworthy again, re-caulking the seams and repairing spars and sails. I assisted several days in hoisting out the iron ballast from the keel and replacing it with heavy stones, which might withstand seawater better.

Sometimes I was in the boat-parties that rowed the officers ashore. There was but a small settlement there, a collection of houses and some dockyard buildings, forges, shipwrights and the like. Cape Town was twenty-five miles across the headland, and the Captain went there to see the Governor and other notables, and Mr Christian often went too, for I think he liked to mix with the society there, and parade himself as a gentleman. But this I think became the moment when his friendship with Captain Bligh fell into decline, because to support his excursions to coffee houses and the other entertainments that the place offered, he borrowed money off the Captain, as I heard with my own ears later.

I did not go to Cape Town or dance at balls, in truth after jigging to Byrne's fiddle I was not over-fond of dancing. The white people were mostly Dutch, and not very friendly, but there was a tavern there which provided a welcome. Quintal said he had been with a Hottentot woman, but I know not if he was just boasting, and I was not minded to sample one myself. He said she smelled like a wet horse.

From Simon's Bay we sailed east, chased onwards by those relentless strong winds from the west, which piled up the seas behind us. It was only two days or so into this voyage when I was at the wheel and heard the Captain in conversation with Mr Christian, who declared what a fine time he had in Cape Town. He wondered how long it might be before he again had the society of such gentry, and supposed that would be in Kingston, Jamaica.

"Well sir," barked the Captain, "I hope that before the gentry of Kingston, or anywhere, have the pleasure of your company, you will repay what you borrowed off me in Cape Town. I am no rich banker, and can not well afford to pay for your amusements."

Mr Christian walked past me with a face like thunder, and his pride was obviously hurt because Captain Bligh had cast doubt on his ability to sustain the place in society to which he aspired. From then on I believe Mr Christian found it more difficult to reason with the Captain on any matter, as others heard remarks which showed that the Captain never failed to remind him of his debt.

Lionel Pettrick

The seas that pursued us were like mountains, and Ned Young, who had knowledge of these things, explained that the Southern Ocean passes all the way around those latitudes without interruption by any land, so the waters are stirred by relentless winds to a ferocity unknown elsewhere on earth. This was especially so during those months, which though summer in northern latitudes were winter where we were in the south. Sometimes the ship was plunged into waves that came over the fo'c'sle, and others washed over the decks from astern, so the Captain ordered the top-gallant masts to be taken down. This made the ship easier to steer, but going aloft and taking off those masts and delivering them secure on the deck while the ship was pitching and rolling so much was a mighty task which taxed the strength and resolution of us all.

For all that, however, the ship was sound, and though we had soakings and the wind was bitter, we were not so miserable as we were at Cape Horn, for now we progressed many miles daily. We passed an island where the captain thought we might find fresh water, but could not come to anchor because the weather was so bad. We continued, seven weeks in all, until we sighted Van Diemen's Land and came to anchor in a bay named Adventure.

We stayed about two weeks in this place, which I heard had been visited before by Captain Bligh when he was Sailing Master on Captain Cook's voyage. Parties were sent out to re-fill our water barrels and fell timber, but we also had time to fish from the ship, and caught some good rock cod.

There was a strange argument between the Captain and Will Purcell, the carpenter, who was directed to make a saw-pit to supply planks. Mr Bligh said the planks were too roughly made, and the wrong size, and Purcell argued with him, saying the Captain had no cause to find fault, and he knew his business better than the Captain, so was immediately ordered back on board. The carpenter was a Warrant Officer, so could not be flogged, and he was put under the charge of Mr Fryer. Then Mr Fryer complained that the man was insolent and disobedient. The Captain had no other punishment than to confine him until he could be brought to court martial, which he did not want to do, as he could not afford to lose an able-bodied craftsman. So he took statements from witnesses of Purcell's behaviour, and gave orders that he should have no food until he agreed to work. Purcell resumed his duties, but Ned told me he heard the Captain berating Mr Fryer and Mr Christian for failing to exert more discipline.

Nothing else occurred in Adventure Bay although some said they had espied naked savages while ashore. I saw none, though at night I saw fires which must have been made by those people. We set sail again, the last long passage of our voyage to Otaheite which lasted above six weeks.

After some weeks we came again into warmer climes and gentler breezes, but by this time we were again reduced to two-thirds of our bread ration, so we were not happy, also because we were obliged to caper to Byrne's fiddle, and John Mills (that was killed on Pitcairn) and Will Brown refused. The Captain stopped their grog and threated further punishment if they again refused, but they preferred that dreary exercise to the misery of no grog, and complied.

James Valentine died. He was struck down by some infection as we came away from Adventure Bay, and complained of pain in his limbs, with severe boughts of coughing. Then he developed a high fever, and the surgeon Mr Huggan bled him, but that led to his death because the drunken fool wielded the knife badly and the wound festered until his whole body was poisoned and he died.

I loved him as a brother and felt great grief at his passing, and was angry at Huggan, as were others, that our only guardian against sickness was a drunkard and not fit for his post. The Captain was angry too, for Huggan had not told him that James was ill, and it came as a shock when the death was reported to him. The weather was quiet that day, and the whole ship could hear him shouting:

"Huggan, damn you, Valentine was a fine young man that we can ill afford to lose, and I do not care to lose my reputation as a Captain who prizes the welfare of his men because of a piss-brain of a surgeon who can not keep his hands off a bottle. You will drink no more on this voyage, you lob-cock scoundrel."

He then gave orders for the midshipmen to search Huggan's cabin and take away all the bottles of spirits and wine that they found. Ned told me that the place was filthy, and he had a considerable store of bottles.

After that, Huggan was no longer invited to dine with the Captain. But he took his revenge, for when men reported some ailment, however slight, he recorded it as 'scurvy', and there were some who were not really sick but went to the surgeon and he recorded them as suffering the same way. So he tried to damage Bligh's reputation, because the Captain was a disciple of Captain Cook and prided himself on preventing the disease of scurvy. In truth by this time the health and strength of most of us was diminished because of our reduced rations, and though the Captain suspected that the symptoms were not so bad as to merit such a diagnosis, he dared not challenge the opinion of one qualified in the profession.

The Captain and Mr Fryer had another disagreement, which we knew about because we were mustered and the Captain read the Article of War concerning the punishment of anyone who disobeys any lawful command. Then he motioned at some of the ship's books and said,

"Sign these books, Mr Fryer, or express your reasons why not at the bottom of the page."

Mr Fryer stepped slowly forward and signed, and said something which we could not hear. Ned said he meant he was signing under protest; but these books were the accounts and records of stores which the Master was required to sign regularly, unless he had proof they were not true. So if Mr Fryer had signed, then he had no proof of a misdeed, and although we could not know what passed between the two of them, it was said that Mr Fryer had sought some favour or recommendation from the Captain in return for signing, which he would not grant.

Thus it was that in those last days of that voyage there was discontent between the Captain and most of the officers, and because of that the crew grew more fractious also, and I sometimes wonder whether there might soon have been a mutiny, had we not first come to Otaheite.

Chapter 9 - Otaheite

When others speak of Paradise and what they have seen there, and you do not yet know it, the senses can not conjure the wonder of such a place as Otaheite. Under a bright sun and a gentle breeze we brought the ship past a reef and into a bay called Matavai, where the water was still and clear, and rich green-clothed mountains swept down to lowlands and beaches of fine dark sand. The hearts of all who regarded it, even of common seamen such as me, were transported in awe and joy, though few words were spoken as we backed and filled the sails, preparing to anchor. The months of privations, of stormy seas and meagre rations, and Bligh's harsh tongue at that moment seemed of little consequence.

Now from the shore came many canoes, and I heard the Captain shouting at them that we were 'tayos' from 'Pretanie', meaning 'friends from Britain'. At this they cheered and waved excitedly, and then with great agility swarmed up the sides and onto the ship, and though the Captain shouted at us to stop them, we could not as they came in such numbers. So he now gave the order to let go the anchor, as we could no longer take the ship where he wanted.

We were surrounded by a jostling crowd talking in their strange tongue, but smiling and embracing us as though we were long-lost friends, and gifts of cooked meat and coconuts and other fruits were pressed upon us, which were most welcome. Even those who had declared themselves sick and were in the care of the surgeon became whole again as if by a miracle, and joined in the merriment. The men of the island were fine fellows, strong and graceful in their bearing, many of them taller than the largest of us. Some had hair cut short, others wore it long, like a fine wig, or tied it in a bunch on their heads.

The women – ah, those women! So many of them were of a beauty surpassing any lady one might see driving by in a coach in London, and their natural charms could not be rivalled by such common women as were the only ones with whom I had consorted before then. Their complexions varied from fair, as a European, to browner hues attained from working or fishing in the sun, but still exceeding comely. They were not ashamed to expose their limbs, which caused the hearts of many of us to beat faster, and their dark hair was smooth and fine, and decorated with flowers. Their sparkling eyes were wide as those of an innocent child, but seemed also to convey an invitation to pleasure, and it was the eyes of one such maiden that met with mine across the throng, and I resolved to seek her out whenever the chance came.

From that day we stayed nearly half a year at Otaheite, and in those months the crew of the Bounty were transported to a life few had experienced before. No more did we climb aloft to furl sails in a gale, or strain our backs at the pumps, or shiver in a damp fo'c'sle with only a few mouthfuls of dried meat and ship's biscuit to fill our bellies. Though common seamen, we were treated by the natives as a superior tribe with Captain Bligh as our chief, as there were many tribes in those islands, sometimes at war with each other, and we could protect those who made us their friends. Thus we all were welcomed wherever we went, and whether on board or ashore I never ate so well in my life, as we were overwhelmed with gifts of hogs, fish and fowl and the many fruits of the island, including the breadfruit, the reason we came there.

We still kept watches, but our duties were light, and I think the ease of our life diminished the Captain's authority over us, as the officers also were seduced by it. The Captain raged at them all and Ned said he was called a "worthless wretch" for some insignificant failure on his watch. After some men deserted, Bligh summoned all the officers and raged at them so loudly I heard some of it.

"Such neglectful and worthless Petty Officers I believe never was in a ship such as are in this! No orders for a few hours together are obeyed by you, and your conduct in general is so bad that no confidence or trust can be reposed in you. In short, you have driven me to everything but Corporal Punishment and that must follow if you do not improve!"

Before them he had already flogged several hands, of which I was the first, so I was not unhappy that the officers might suffer the same. Our lives of pleasure did not mix with naval discipline, and it seems to me now that by the time we departed we were changed so much that the Captain could no longer force his will on all as he had been used to, and a decision to mutiny was of little consequence to many of us. But though there is much that happened on that island of which I know nothing, I will try to recount what I remember.

When we anchored, a notice was nailed to the mizzenmast which I could not read, but was told that these were orders, firstly not to tell the natives that Captain Cook was dead, or to say the purpose of our visit was to collect breadfruit plants. As I knew little of Captain Cook and nothing of the native tongue, there was little danger that I or my shipmates would betray such secrets. We were to show friendship to the natives and commit no violence against them, and no trade was to be done except through the officer appointed by the Captain, so as not to create unnecessary competition for their wares.

That last injunction was the cause of unrest with the officers, particularly Mr Fryer later on, because a friend brought him the gift of a hog, which the Captain saw and ordered to be added to the ship's stores. Mr Fryer protested angrily that this was not a trade but a gift, and when the fellow that brought it saw the quarrel he jumped overboard taking the carcass with him, which enraged the Captain mightily. However, most of us were little concerned because our bellies were full and the only trade that interested us was a lady's favours, which could be had for a couple of iron nails. In truth, so much iron went out of that ship that I wonder there was any left for the carpenter, or the ship did not fall to pieces.

Iron was as precious to those people as gold is to anyone in Europe, because they had no means of getting it except when ships like ours came, and it served them better for tips to arrows or spears, or for fishhooks, than the flints or shells they had, and they could fashion many other things from a piece of iron such as a knife from the iron band of a cask. They would take it whenever they could, and this was also my undoing. I was set to guard the launch one day, which was moored alongside the ship, and I was sat at the bow exchanging friendly gestures and the few words I had learned with some men and girls in canoes which were there. Most of all I could not take my eyes off Jenny, as I called her, the girl I had seen on deck when we arrived, and I had been with her many times since then, and I loved her dearly. The afternoon passed pleasantly enough, but later on when the launch was required, they could not ship the rudder because the gudgeon pin was missing from the stern.

I was called up before Mr Churchill and required to explain the loss, which I could not, so was paraded before the Captain, who read the Article of War concerning neglect of duty.

"Have you anything to say, Smith?"

I could think of nothing to say which would not enrage the Captain and increase my punishment. I thought only that I had been beaten by Mr Woodlea for stealing food, and sent for a whipping by the Blind Beak for thievery, and now I was to be flogged only because someone else had stolen what was in my care.

"Twelve lashes, Mr Morrison, seize him up."

The native chief was on board with some of his people, and when they saw me being tied to the grating and realised what was occurring they let out a cry, the women especially. I think the chief, whose name was Tynah, tried to dissuade Bligh from such harshness, but he was ignored, and most of his people departed, unwilling to witness it.

As the cat bit into my back, I thought only of Jenny. Her real name was "Teehutea" or some such. I met her when I first went with a shore party, and we were all like dogs straining at the leash, looking around everywhere as we walked off the beach and towards a spit of land which Mr Christian said was 'Point Venus', a name which further fired our imagination. It was there the Captain had ordered a shelter to be erected where the breadfruit plants might be collected and prepared for shipment. After some preparatory work, only an hour or two, for Mr Christian was no hard task-master, we sat down in some shade and I was resting my back against a tree when I felt a tap on my shoulder. I turned round, and there she was! She beckoned and I scrambled behind her into some undergrowth, then she held out her arms to me.

Ah, I had never know such delight! She revealed her body to me without shame, and I thought that place was justly named after Venus, because that girl was as beautiful as any goddess. She smelled so sweet and pure, and what we did together seemed no sin, just two young lovers giving pleasure to each other, a world away from those grim couplings with the doxies of Newcastle and London.

Afterwards she sat up with a whistful little smile and held out her hand. I assumed she sought payment, and I had some nails in my pocket from the work we were doing, which I gave to her. She laughed, and gestured to herself, saying her "Tee" name that I mentioned before. This was too difficult for me, so I said "You – Jenny."

"Jen-i" she repeated, understanding that was my name for her, then I gestured at myself.

"Alex"

"Arets" she repeated, giggling.

"Smith, where the hell are you?" - Mr Christian had finally realised he was a man short. I bade farewell to my sweetheart and stepped from the bushes.

"Sorry sir, call of nature."

"Very well, Smith, too many peaches, I'll be bound," he replied with a wink. We ate no peaches on Otaheite, but Mr Christian was himself sampling the local delicacies, as we all knew.

In truth the natives were as determined and adept at thievery as any that I had known on the streets of London. No doubt they would say it was no great sin to steal from the ship, indeed they maybe thought it was no sin at all, as their ideas of right and wrong were different from ours. In London I stole from the necessity of keeping body and soul together, but when I was tempted to try for more than that, I was led into murder. At Otaheite the people had enough for a comfortable life whether we were there or not, so I can not say they had any need to steal from us, though there was no loss to myself, and I thought of it as a sport to catch or prevent them.

The Captain, however, was much exercised by any loss from the ship, and never failed to punish someone if he thought they should have prevented it. The Chief also did not encourage stealing, and after the first theft, of a tin pot, the miscreant was nearly killed by his own people. However, those clever people lost no opportunity to take the smallest hook or thimble, and the Captain soon forbade any of them to come on board, except the Chiefs whom he welcomed almost daily. Even an anchor buoy was taken, I suppose for the iron hoops, although some parts were later recovered.

Later on Rob the Butcher got a dozen lashes after his cleaver was stolen (although it was brought back later), and Will Muspratt got the same because he let something go. Also the rudder from one of the boats was taken from the tent ashore, but I do not think anyone was flogged for that, although the Captain could be heard in furious discourse with Mr Christian.

I believe that by now there was no close friendship between Captain Bligh and Mr Christian, who spent nearly all his time ashore in charge of the party assisting the gardeners to collect and cultivate the breadfruit plants. This work continued steadily, and was not difficult, so all the party had enough opportunity to pursue amours with those lovely women, as they did not come on board after their work, and were free to spend the night where they willed. I was not one of that party, but had many occasions to go ashore for other duties, cutting timber or gathering stores for the ship, so it was not difficult to slip away to spend sweet moments with Jenny. Indeed, the Captain did not forbid ladies to come aboard at night, and in the darkness of the fo'c'sle could be heard many tender noises and sighs from all the couples that were there. It was also wonderful to sit on deck in the stillness with the vast starry heaven above, looking at the lights of boats fishing out on the reef.

The surgeon Huggan died. The removal of his supply of spirits during the voyage had not lessened his craving or his ability to satisfy it, because the natives make a strong drink from a root called 'yava', and he had his fill of that. They took him to be buried on Point Venus, but I asked to be given a duty on the ship, as I did not want to go. I did not mourn for him, and felt no regret, only satisfaction that the dissoluteness which had led to the death of poor James had brought about his end also.

In the last months of that year the weather became stormy, with much rain, and large waves came over the reef, making the anchorage unsafe. The gardeners also were concerned that strong winds across Point Venus were driving salt spray which would damage the plants, so the Captain ordered the ship to be moved to a more sheltered anchorage. Then we made a new shelter nearby and afterwards moved all the plants from Point Venus.

It was Christmas day when we moved the ship, and I thought about the Christmas before, when we had just broken free of England and I was not long free of the difficulties I had before. I felt happy now, happier than I ever had been, and wished I could continue as I was for ever.

The young men and women and the children of Pitcairn know little of the customs of Otaheite and observe the Scriptures rather than the rituals of their mothers' people. Even now, what I remember of those rituals seems strange.

Tynah, the Chief, came almost daily to dine with the Captain. He was a mountain of a man, tall and very powerful, and his wife, called Ideeah, was also big and quite handsome, and much younger than him. I did not see this because I was not present, but I heard that the Chief would never touch the food himself, instead had a servant put the food or drink in his mouth, and on occasion the Captain would raise the cup to his lips. Ideeah would never take her food with him, but always separately afterwards, which was the custom of all the people, as we saw when we went to their houses, that a husband would have a separate place to eat from his wife.

Tynah and his people showed us great friendship, and we were welcomed into their houses, and sometimes to their feasts, when there was music from drums and flutes, and a dance they called 'heiva'. This was performed by young men and women, with many wanton gestures and distortion of their faces, and whether it was for them a religious festival or merely for enjoyment I know not, but we sailors enjoyed the spectacle. There was wrestling, too, and Quintal tried his luck against a lad little more than a boy but soon found himself on his back to great laughter by all, so none of us were so bold after that.

The island was formed like two mountains, a greater and a lesser joined by a narrow low-lying strip of land, the length of the two together maybe forty miles, I was told. This was inhabited by different tribes, all with their own Chiefs, and the Captain entertained many of them, as well as Chiefs from other islands. There was also a society, with members from many tribes, who considered themselves superior, I think a little like the lords and ladies of England, and they were called Aree-oy. The young Aree-oy prided themselves as warriors and had licence to roam in bands, taking anything they wanted, and the men made free with any woman they chose. But here is a terrible thing, as if any woman of lesser birth had a child by an Aree-oy it must be instantly killed, and sometimes Aree-oy women also killed their babies. I heard tell of one Chief and his wife, both Aree-oy, who killed all the eight children they had, yet adopted a nephew as their heir, and loved him greatly. I can hardly understand how such wicked customs can be acceptable to any human being, even those who have not received the Word of Our Lord.

The children that were allowed to live were well-treated, and could be seen flying kites, jumping in a rope, walking on stilts or wrestling "just like any child in England", as I heard Captain Bligh remark, though I never remember such pleasures in my childhood. I looked at those children and wondered if they in turn would grow up to kill babies, and as I watch our children playing on Pitcairn I thank God that they will never know such things.

The people detested incest as much as any Christian, but their code permitted connections that would be frowned on in English society. A man's close friendship with another would give him licence to lie with that man's wife, but with no other member of that family, as the man having been accepted into that family, this would be regarded as incest. It was also common for brothers to enjoy each others' wives, though strangers who sought the privilege would be violently rejected.

Jenny told me, by gestures, still our main means of communication, that the servant who fed Chief Tynah was also the paramour of his wife Ideeah, but Tynah knew of it and did not mind.

"Inclination seems to be the only law of marriage at Otaheite," I heard Mr Christian saying to the Captain, and laughing.

"Indeed sir, I must take a note of that," Bligh replied.

Jenny was still inclined toward me, and Mr Christian had not failed to pursue his inclinations, but I do not think the Captain ever did, if he had any.

The Captain made a strange attempt to entertain a party that came on board one evening. One of the hands, Dick Skinner, who took the ship with us, was also the barber, and had brought with him a painted head such as hairdressers have in their shop to show the different fashions of dressing hair. The face was well-made, and Bligh had it mounted on a frame with a wig and clothing, so that in the dim evening light it could easily be taken for a real person. He then pointed it out to his guests, saying that he had an Englishwoman on board. This deceived many, and one old woman rushed to make obeisance to the figure, with gifts of fruit and cloth. Finally the deception was revealed, and the Chiefs enjoyed the joke, but the old woman was mortified and quickly took her gifts back. Maybe the Captain did not intend it so, but it is a mean act, to cause simple kindly people to be mocked.

It was the custom for the people of Otaheite to be tattooed, mainly on their buttocks, although the men also have it on their legs, and Aree-oy men over the entire lower part of their body, to above the waist. I was tattooed as you can still see, and most of the crew also had some to their own design, or in the native style, as did Mr Christian. The ink was just a paste of soot and water, and they pierced the skin with needles made of hog's teeth, which was exceedingly painful, though not so much as being flogged.

Apart from those already mentioned, two other men were

flogged, one of them was Isaac Martin, the American, for beating one of the natives, but then the deserters were also flogged. I think they were mad to run for it as they did, but there were few of us in the fo'c'sle who did not think about doing the same, and whispered it to those they trusted. A group of us were ashore one evening, drinking 'yava' with our girls close by.

"Well, how many more evenings will we have like this?" said young Tom Ellison, "we're nearly three months here now."

"Billy Brown was saying that their plants are nearly ready, " I said, "and when the weather turns favourable we're likely to be off."

"Back with that old bastard and his oaths and half-rations, and more floggings, I'll be bound," said Quintal, "my back pains me when I think of all that."

"I was having the exact same conversation a day ago," said John Millward, "with Will Muspratt and Churchill. We reckon if we got to one of the other islands and bargained with the natives for a canoe to go further, Bligh would never find us."

"What, the Corporal wants to run?" exclaimed Quintal, "and he could get arms, too!"

"Aye," said John, "then we can defend ourselves if the natives are not friendly. Will wants no more of Bligh's 'Bounty' after the flogging he had, and Chas and I would rather take a chance on staying in these islands than suffer a miserable voyage back to England." He looked round at us. "I trust you to say nothing to anyone, but if you want to come with us, you should say so now."

We looked at him and at each other, but said nothing, and the very next night they were gone, with some arms and ammunition and one of the boats. This was not discovered till the morning, because the Officer of the Watch who should have stopped them was Midshipman Tom Hayward, who was asleep on duty, for which the penalty is hanging. He was instantly disrated, and clapped in irons.

Bligh sought the help of the Chiefs to find the deserters, and the boat was found at Matavai Bay, where we were before. They had followed the plan told to us by Millward and sailed away in a canoe, heading for islands many leagues to the north.

In Churchill's possessions the Captain found a paper naming Mr Christian and others on the shore party, and he questioned them all closely, but they swore they had no knowledge of Churchill's plan, so the matter was dropped. I can not think why Churchill would name these people, unless he had mentioned his plan to them and hoped they would come with him.

About three weeks later there came information that the men had come back to an island about six miles away, and the Captain led a party to apprehend them. They were brought back the next day, a sorry sight, and John Millward would not meet my eye as he came aboard in chains. They were sentenced to two dozen lashes, which was repeated a few weeks later, when Hayward was released from irons and restored to duty.

"Well, there it is for all of ye now," sneered Byrne after the first flogging, "if ye want to desert or mutiny, it needs more than three of yez."

That unpleasant man spoke no more or less than the truth.

Chapter 10 – Farewell to Otaheite

In those final weeks at the island, the pleasant life we had enjoyed there was marred by the knowledge that it was coming to an end. Bill Brown said there were close on one thousand breadfruit plants in their garden, and they were soon to be transferred to the ship. At this time someone cut the anchor cable a little below the water-line nearly all the way through, so that if it had parted the ship must have been driven on to the reef. We supposed this must have been done by someone who did not want us to leave, but we never discovered whether that was one of the ship's company or a native. While I spliced in a new length of rope I thought of dear old Morgan and the fishermen who taught me the art.

The thieving continued or even increased because the natives knew such opportunities were soon to end. One dark night a water-cask and a compass, with some other articles, were stolen from the shore-station, giving the Captain cause for another outburst of rage at the Officers. He went to Tynah and demanded that the thief be produced. The poor wretch was soon brought to the ship with the compass, and Tynah told the Captain he should shoot him. A hundred lashes was the punishment, far more than was given to any of us, and he was then put in irons below, but he soon broke the shackle and then jumped overboard and swam away.

"God damn you sir, I should have you flogged," Bligh raged at the mate of the watch, George Stewart. The Captain stamped around the deck cursing the neglectfulness of his officers and complaining that they all needed constantly reminding of their duty.

Pitcairn's Father

But now the time came when all the plants we had come for, and all the stores, were loaded on the ship, and we must endure the tearful partings from our sweethearts. Jenny clung to me weeping bitterly, and a mournful chorus of sighs and sobbing could be heard from the shadows all around. She whispered to me words that clearly meant I should not go, she would hide me somewhere, and I was sorely tempted, God knows, I did not want to leave her. But I knew that Bligh would have any deserter hunted down by Tynah, and the punishment would be severe. This must have been the thought of us all, because when we were ordered aboard that night, no man was missing.

The next day we worked the ship out through the reef, followed by many canoes, and I spied Jenny holding out her arms towards me, as did a host of the beauties who had brought such bliss into our lives, as they sang a slow mournful song. The Captain said goodbye to Tynah and Ideeah, presenting them with some arms and ammunition and receiving in return a quantity of coconuts to add to the great mass of stores which were everywhere in the ship. Then we set sail and left them, and when we got so far we could no longer distinguish any person or hear their cries, Byrne struck up the tune that the girls had sung on his fiddle. I thought to curse him and tell him to stop, because I am sure he did it to mock us over what we were losing, but I just listened, because it was a sweet tune.

Our course was now towards the west, and we passed the last of the Society Islands. A few days later we came to an island which interested the Captain and he had us sail all the way round it. Some natives came out in canoes and we hove to for more than a day while the Captain parleyed and traded with them, but we did not go ashore. Sailing further, one day in light winds and clear weather the lookout shouted a warning about a column of water that was rushing towards us.

"A waterspout!" exclaimed the Captain, and ordered the helm hard over, and the sails reefed, so the spout rushed some yards astern of us and we suffered no damage.

"Had it hit us directly I fear it would have brought down the masts," he remarked to Mr Fryer.

Continuing a few more days we sighted more islands, which Ned said were called the Friendly Islands. I wonder how they came to be so named because the natives were not so friendly as those on Otaheite, and it was here that any friendship there had been between Captain Bligh and Mr Christian was destroyed. There were sudden changes in the weather before we came to those islands, and one night on Mr Christian's watch there was a squall, so that the sails were backed by a violent wind which put the ship in irons, and all hands were called to reef, and to brace the yards, to get the ship under way again. The Captain came on deck and cursed Mr Christian for an incompetent fool who would destroy us all. I never heard Mr Christian raise his voice as much before, but he screamed at the Captain, and was heard throughout the ship.

"Sir, you see how dark it is and there was no warning. Your abuse is so bad that I can not do my duty with any pleasure. I have been in hell for weeks with you!"

We looked at each other and shook our heads. How could these two men remain at close quarters on this vessel for the many months and many thousands of miles before this voyage was complete?

We came to an island where Bligh wanted to stay because he had been there before with Captain Cook. Parties were sent ashore to get wood and water, and the natives we saw there were sickly and deformed, not at all like the people on Otaheite, and they were not friendly either. All the while we were there they never stopped trying to steal from us, and waved their spears and clubs when we resisted. The Captain had ordered muskets to be sent in the boat, but kept there and only be shown, not used, so the men felling the timber or taking the barrels must watch each other all the time, and the work was done very slowly. Matt Quintal had to jump on a savage that was brandishing a club behind Mr Fryer, and narrowly saved him from being struck down.

"For God's sake, why doesn't he just shoot one of the wretches?" grunted Quintal, as we rolled barrels under a hail of stones.

Mr Christian reported these attacks to the Captain, who jeered "Damn you for a cowardly rascal, Mr Christian, are you afraid of a set of naked savages while you are armed?"

"The arms are no use while your orders prevent them being used," Christian retorted, turning on his heel.

The natives also succeeded in stealing the iron grapnel from one of the boats, by going underwater and holding the line tight until another had untied the grapnel and swum away with it. The Captain cursed all who had gone ashore for allowing this to happen, and as there were some of the chiefs on board with him, he detained them and said the ship would sail with them if the grapnel was not returned. After some hours, and it was not returned, the people started crying and cutting themselves, so the Captain gave in and let them go. All of us who had been threatened by spears and hit by stones were unhappy that the Captain seemed not to care for our protection, while he tried to find favour with the Chiefs of those savages.

Chapter 11 – Mutiny!

I could say that Captain Bligh lost the 'Bounty' because he raged about coconuts, although that would only be the last of his scornful rages, of which I have already recounted much. It was some days after we had left that island and we were approaching another which was topped by a volcano, a wonderful sight at night from many miles distant, sending a pillar of fire into the sky.

It was a calm day and the ship was making very little way when I noticed the Captain on deck inspecting a pile of coconuts, for there was so much produce and livestock aboard that some of it was stored on deck, and even in the ship's boats. Then all the officers were seen running to their quarters , and fetching out coconuts and showing them to the captain. He finished by shouting at them all, and then retired to his cabin. Ned told me that Bligh was accusing them of stealing his coconuts, and had ordered their grog to be stopped, and their portions of yams to be halved. Mr Christian had objected to the Captain's accusation, but Bligh had cursed him as a "damned hound", and said he'd be "done with you all" after the ship had come through the Endeavour Straits, past New Holland.

Ned said he did not know what Bligh meant by that, if he did mean anything at all, but all the officers were now very ill at ease, and resentful at his arbitrary reduction in their allowances, and below decks we also fell to wondering whether our grog or yams would be stopped. Now the ship was in a ferment of whispering and wondering what would next befall us, and I was sitting that evening with a few others when Isaac Martin, the American, came down.

"Can you imagine this?" he whispered, "Mr Christian is building a raft! He means to leave the ship. He is in such distress after Bligh accused him of stealing, on top of all the other insults, he says he can not remain any more."

"What madness," said Quintal, "where would he go? He'd likely drown in the first squall, or if he gets ashore anywhere the natives will knock him on the head."

"Aye," said another, "and all that is if Bligh doesn't hunt him down like a dog, which he would surely want to do."

"Well," said Martin, "I was there with that young midshipman Stewart, and we both said as much to him. But his eyes were wild, like a cornered animal, and I can not see how he and Bligh can stay together another few days, let alone many months. Then Stewart said to him 'Why not take the ship?'"

"That boy is a mischief-maker," I said.

"Aye" said Martin, "but when he said it, Christian just looked at him, then at the raft, and then he said he could not take the ship on his own. George Stewart said that the crew liked him and were tired of Bligh and his rages, and many wanted to go back to Otaheite. He looked at me and I said it was true, and many would follow his lead."

"I was in a mutiny where a man was killed," I said, "and I'll take no part in another one where any blood is shed."

The discussion continued for a short while, but all were cautious about committing themselves to any firm action lest one of us might disagree and betray us. But I sensed that if Mr Christian started it, we would have a mutiny. Myself, I thought no good would come of it, and in my mind's eye saw again the 'Penelope' and Redepath falling dead upon the deck. I had fled and joined the 'Bounty' to escape such chaos and evil, but it was pursuing me to the other side of the world. I slept little that night.

The following day the ship was almost becalmed in light airs, and the distant volcano was quiet, like the mood on board, where all went about their duties with downcast eyes and little in the way of conversation. There were no eruptions from the Captain either, but I noticed that Mr Christian would do no more than acknowledge his orders, and would scarcely meet his eye. Presently the Captain went below, then I saw Chas Churchill approach Mr Christian and they spoke together for ten minutes or more. Next, Churchill went to some of the men on deck and then disappeared below, but soon came out again and up on the foredeck where I was patching a sail.

"Alex," he said," Christian is minded to take the ship and put Bligh and anyone who resists us ashore somewhere. Are you with us?"

I hesitated, uncertain still that I should put myself on the wrong side of the law yet again.

"Come, man, can't you see that it is impossible for Bligh and Christian to exist together for another twelve days, never mind twelve months or however long this voyage lasts? Think you that Bligh will become kinder to us all as we go on, or how many more times will he cut our rations or stop our grog? He will not finish this voyage without some more disaster, and if something must be done, 'twere better done now, as we can easily go back to Otaheite, which is what many of us want, and I'll lay you do too. Bligh flogged us both, in your case for very little reason, we don't owe him any loyalty, he seems to despise everybody. There are enough of us to do this, so will you join us?"

"But how shall it be done?"

"We wait for Christian. He'll have the second watch in the morning, and enough of his men are with him. They have to get the key to the arms chest, and keep the other officers out of the way. Then they can arrest Bligh. What do you say?"

"I'll commit violence against no man."

"There should be no violence. Most of the hands are with us, and you know the officers, they've barely a spine between them. If we take Bligh, we take the ship."

"Aye, well, I'd rather go back to Otaheite than be flogged again."

"Good man. It's all on Mr Christian, we take our chances with him if or when he gives the order. Just wait for a signal."

And so it happened. I was off watch and in my hammock that night, unable to sleep as I thought of what was to come, and also imagined myself back in the arms of my sweet Jenny. But it was from a dream that I was awakened in the darkness by a hand shaking my shoulder and a voice said "Turn to, the game has started." I hastened on deck to see a huge pillar of fire from the volcano, angry once again, and the first glimmer of dawn astern. There was Mr Christian, his eyes ablaze, brandishing a pistol and a bayonet, with a group of men beside him. A pistol was thrust into my hand.

"Chas, Jack, Tom, Alex, John, Matt, come with me. You others guard the hatchways, let no-one come out."

We descended the aft hatchway to Bligh's cabin, and John Sumner, Matt Quintal and I were ordered to remain outside and stand guard over Mr Fryer's cabin, which was opposite. The others went in to Bligh, and I saw Tom Burkitt place the flat of a cutlass across his chest as he lay in his cot, while Christian put a hand on him and told him to make no noise. The Captain did not obey, and set up an almighty cry of "Murder!" as they hauled him out of the cot in his nightshirt and bound his hands behind his back. The noise roused other officers, but they found sentries at their doors and remained where they were. As the Captain was led on deck Mr Fryer attempted to follow him, but Matt said he'd shoot him if he did not remain where he was and keep quiet.

For a while I was still on guard below, but I could hear the Captain on deck bellowing in anger, and also the jeers of some of my fellow mutineers;

"Damn his eyes, put him in a boat and let the bugger see if he can live off half a pound of yams a day!"

"You brought this on yourself, Bligh!"

"Why, a boat is too good for him, let him swim!"

Fryer was then allowed on deck, but after some fruitless attempts to reason with Mr Christian, who said it was "too late", he was sent back to his cabin. John Sumner remained below on guard over him.

Now there was much coming and going on deck, as Mr Christian ordered the cutter to be launched, in which he thought to send away the Captain with Mr Samuel, his clerk, and two of the Midshipmen, Hayward and Hallett. However, the Boatswain and others protested that they might as well be thrown into the sea, because the bottom of that boat was so rotten that it was already sinking. Thus the larger launch was lowered, and I think Mr Christian was a little taken aback when it became clear that many were willing to go in the boat, more than it would hold.

The only Able Seaman not with us was the fiddler Byrne, and he made a show of wanting to go in the boat but was stopped. Those who were to be cast away did not relish his company any more than we did. Samuel, Hayward and Hallett were gradually joined in the boat by Ledward (who became Surgeon after Huggan died), the Boatswain, the Mate, Peckover the Gunner, both Quartermasters, Bligh's steward, the Chief Gardener, and some others. Will Purcell the Carpenter started to climb down, which was a surprise because he had openly defied the Captain before, and been punished for it. Mr Christian at first stopped him, thinking his skills would be needed on the ship, but then let him go because the man was such a contumelious character that it was better if he went. Then Purcell started shouting for his toolbox, and someone shouted back, "Nay, give him that and he'll build another ship!" Mr Christian ordered his box to be given him so that he would go quietly.

Pitcairn's Father

Mr Christian ordered a double serving of grog to all who had mutinied, which provoked a great cheer from all of us. Mr Fryer was brought from his cabin and ordered into the boat. Bligh called out to him to stay, but Christian motioned him with his bayonet toward the ladder, and he went.

Finally there were eighteen men already in the launch, which was no more than twenty-three feet long and seven feet wide, laden with supplies of bread, pork, rum and water, and some of Bligh's papers which Samuel had collected, along with a compass and almanack, but no charts. Then Mr Christian turned to Mr Bligh.

"Come, Captain Bligh, your officers and men are now in the boat and you must go with them."

"Is this treatment a proper return for the many instances you have received of my friendship?" asked Bligh sorrowfully as he was led to the ladder, "Consider, Fletcher Christian, I have a wife and four children in England, and you have danced my children upon your knee."

"That, Captain Bligh, is the thing, I am in hell – I am in hell."

I believe that Fletcher Christian truly was in hell at that moment, and the poor fellow never escaped.

By the ladder as the Captain went down was a small group, calling out to him. These were Coleman, the Armourer, and the Carpenter's Mates Tom McIntosh and Charles Norman, as well as Michael Byrne, who all sought to assure Bligh that they had played no part in the mutiny and wished to go with him. But most of us were also at the side, jeering and laughing, with cries of "Shoot the bugger!" "A quarter pound of yams a day!" "Stop his grog!" and the like. Bligh looked up and roared,

"Never fear my lads, I'll do you justice if ever I get to England!" Whether he meant us or Coleman and the others I know not.

The launch was then veered astern and four cutlasses were handed down before it was cast off. Then Mr Christian ordered Tom Ellison aloft to unfurl the topsail, and slowly the launch and the ship moved apart. I was standing at the taffrail when I heard the windows of the Great Cabin below being opened, and then splashes, as a line of breadfruit plants bobbed in our wake.

"Take 'em in tow, Cap'n. If they thrive in seawater you won't go hungry!" - then cackling laughter. Bligh shook his head in disbelief, and turned away.

"Huzza for Otaheite!" shouted someone.

"Huzza for Otaheite indeed," said Ned Young, who had appeared at my side. "A warm day's work, and all before breakfast."

"Why, Ned, I did not see you earlier."

"I was asleep when you took Bligh, and the guards would not let me out on deck before most of the business was done."

"So you did not expect this, then."

"In truth I expected something, because Christian has been boiling like yon volcano for days. I made him the suggestion that he seek the support of all the officers to detain Bligh and make a case against him before the Admiralty with all their grievances – but he can not have done so, as you see most of them now in that boat with him."

"Aye, and they made no resistance to us at all, except maybe Fryer, they meekly followed each other into the boat. They are like a flock of sheep that has been harried by the dog for weeks and no longer know where to turn without it. But you were not minded to go with them?"

"Nay, I lost all respect for Bligh after he called me a 'filthy mulatto'. There may be few who can live up to his standards of perfection, but he is so immoderate in his rage that his authority is defiled. In any case, who are more likely to be alive two months from now, you and I, or Mr Bligh's flock?"

"The boat has less than eight inches of freeboard, so may sink in the first squall, and they have provisions and water for about five days. I fancy the 'Bounty' will stay afloat longer than that."

"There's your answer, then. It will be months before the 'Bounty' is missed, and much longer before anyone comes in pursuit of us. If they find us we will surely hang, so we must use these months to find a safe place, which can not be Otaheite."

"Do you think that Christian has a plan?" I asked.

"I do not know. I'm sure Bligh has," replied Ned with a laugh. "Come, let us see what we can find for breakfast, as the cook and the butcher have resigned."

He gestured at the launch, now a mile or two away from us. The figures in it were now indistinct, the faces I had seen daily for more than eighteen months I would never see again. I was one of those responsible for that disappearing speck of humanity that might be snuffed out in a few days. When they stood in front of me I could not have stuck any of them with a bayonet or put a bullet in them, but as that speck disappeared I did not care what happened to it. Nobody cared. It was a wicked thing we did that day.

Chapter 12 - Tubuai

With the ship under way for nearly an hour, Mr Christian summoned everyone, twenty-four of us, to the quarterdeck and addressed us;

"Men, now we have taken the ship we can have no rest until we find a place where the Navy will not find us. That may take many weeks' sailing until we are settled, and the ship must be worked like any other. I offer myself as Captain, if you will have me."

"Why not, ye can be the first to hang!" shouted Byrne. All ignored him, and there was a brief awkward silence.

"Aye, Mr Christian, we'll follow you come hell or high water!" shouted someone.

"He's in hell already, he said so to Captain Bligh," sneered Byrne.

Churchill seized Byrne by his collar and flung him to the deck.

"One more word from you and your fiddle goes over the side, and your Irish arse after it!" he roared.

"As to hell," rejoined Christian, "I am already relieved of the torment visited on me daily by Captain Bligh, as are you all. If you will give me a show of hands, I will serve as your Captain."

I raised my hand as did most of us, although those who had sought to get into the boat, Coleman, McIntosh and Norman, as well as Byrne and Morrison, did not.

"Very well, we must divide into two watches. I will lead one, George Stewart the other. I do not wish to clap anyone in irons, so I hope that those of you who did not raise your hands just now will play your part and work with the rest of us."

None dissented, so he continued;

"There is an island named Tubuai about one hundred leagues south of Otaheite, which we could look to as our home - "

"That is not right or fair, Mr Christian," piped up young Peter Heywood, "we must stay in Otaheite, so that those who did not mutiny can have the justice that Captain Bligh promised us."

"Hah, the mouse roars," scoffed Churchill, accompanied by much jeering, "I saw you on the foredeck laughing at Bligh in his nightshirt. D'ye think they'll spare you the rope?"

"Churchill, you may not address a Midshipman in such a manner!" squealed Heywood.

"Peter, you are no longer a Midshipman in the Royal Navy," said Christian, raising a calming hand, "we are all now just pirates. And as to Bligh's justice, whatever part anyone played, or did not, in taking the ship, do you think that boat will still be afloat in two days, or two weeks, or two months time, or anyone in it left alive to tell what happened today? Because if they do not live, and the Navy finds you, whatever tale you tell there will be no evidence to confirm that you were any less of a mutineer than I. So you are trusting your plan to eight inches of freeboard and the friendship of the natives wherever they go ashore. Better to trust your luck with us, lad, and heed my plan."

Even the dissenters accepted Mr Christian's argument, and there was no further quarrel. He explained that Tubuai was shown on the chart, but few ships had ever stopped there, and ships did not normally pass that way. There was an anchorage within a reef, but it was not well surveyed. If we could establish a refuge there, we could then visit Otaheite to collect such friends and women as would come with us and return to Tubuai. This was accepted by all, and we set sail for Tubuai.

The voyage lasted four weeks, and there was an uneasy peace

on board during that time. Initially there was some taunting of Bligh's "loyalists" by some of the more excited mutineers, and Mr Christian had to bid them cease their mockery, but it died away as all realised how uncertain was our future, and wondered whether we had done the right thing. Mr Christian set us to sewing uniform shirts made from old sails, as he said the natives were always impressed by such uniforms.

Ned Young was drafted to George Stewart's watch, as was I, so we now had frequent discussions together. I think Mr Christian trusted both of us to support George in case any thought to rise against him. I certainly had suspicions about Morrison (the Boatswain's Mate who had flogged me), because I had seen him exchanging words with Fryer during the mutiny, and I thought he would seek an opportunity to retake the ship. Christian now kept the key to the arms chest, and issued weapons to all whom he considered loyal, including myself. We never left Jim Morrison alone for long, and I think he had little support for an uprising then.

Finally we hove to off Tubuai, and I was with the party in the cutter led by George Stewart to seek out the entrance to the reef, last described by Captain Cook. We were taking soundings in the opening when a canoe came out with natives brandishing spears. They came close, so close they could not easily use their spears, but they clearly meant to do us harm, and George loosed off a brace of pistols at them. Only one worked at all, and that was a misfire, but it served to scare off our attackers. We returned to the ship.

"Is this the place where we are to live a life of peace, harmony and freedom?" Ned Young wondered.

Our first visit to Tubuai could hardly be deemed a success. The following morning we worked the ship in through the reef and anchored in a sandy, quite shallow bay. Now we were surrounded by native canoes, which paddled round the ship all day, but none would accept our invitations to come aboard. The next day an old man did come on board, and we thought he must be their chief. His only purpose, however, must have been to spy on us, but we were greatly amused when he jumped back in fright at the sight of our animals, as it seemed he had never seen a hog or a dog before. Mr Christian then gave him some presents and he departed.

Some hours later more canoes approached, including one in which about twenty young women were singing and swaying their bodies in a lascivious manner. We all raised a cheer and beckoned them on board.

"A real welcome at last," laughed Quintal.

"Look to your weapons, men!" shouted Mr Christian, "see how many canoes come with them!"

The women came on board and we gave them trinkets, but after them swarmed several dozen men who tried to steal anything that was not fixed down. Mr Christian caught a man trying to steal the card out of the compass, and flogged him with a rope's end. We followed his example and began to drive them off the ship with pistol butts, marlin spikes or anything that came to hand. Gradually they all left, the women with them.

Once back in their canoes, the men produced spears and clubs and brandished them with real menace. One man cut away the anchor buoy and Mr Christian fired a musket at him, and ordered one of the cannon to be fired. At this all the canoes retreated to the shore, and our boats were launched to follow them. As we came up to the beach we were met with a hail of stones, and they charged towards us. We raised our muskets but they did not stop, so we fired. Several fell, and they turned tail and disappeared into the wood. A few wounded staggered after them, but three or four lay dead on the beach.

"We had none of this at Matavai Bay," I remarked with sorrow.

"Indeed, I would rather name this Bloody Bay," replied Ned.

To discourage further attacks we rafted all the canoes together and towed them out to the ship, but they broke away during the night and drifted back to the shore. The next morning Mr Christian led two parties in the boats to seek peace with the natives, but there were none to be seen. We landed in several places on that side of the island, and left gifts such as hatchets and knives by their houses, but no-one approached us.

The following morning a boat was sent ashore again, but there was no-one to be found. Mr Christian then mustered us on deck.

"Now I have the measure of this place I think the time is right to make for Otaheite."

A rousing cheer went up from all.

"My plan remains the same. We will obtain adequate numbers of livestock, for there appear to be none here, and then return, with such of your friends or women that wish to come with you."

There was much murmuring and unrest when he said that.

"After what has passed these two days you will still prefer Bloody Bay to Matavai Bay?" said Jim Morrison with disbelief.

"Yes Jim, the reasons being the same as before. It is certain the Navy will go back to Otaheite, and if they find you, you will almost certainly hang. It might be many long years, if ever, before another ship comes here. The natives are not friendly at present, but I believe we can win them round, as Captain Cook once did those on Otaheite. This island is not large, and I think the population is not either, so we should not be overwhelmed before we bring them to friendship."

"Mr Christian, I do not believe the natives here are as amenable as those on Otaheite," said Morrison.

"Be that as it may, we have the force of arms and can organise to resist them until they decide to live in peace with us. All I now desire is to live here in peace."

If men still harboured doubts they did not utter them, and as we weighed anchor and put out to sea, the spirits of all were lifted at the prospect of seeing Otaheite again.

A few days later, with Otaheite in sight, Mr Christian summoned all on deck and addressed us;

"When Tynah and the people meet us they will want to know where are Bligh and the others, why we have come back, and where the plants are, as they will know we could not have delivered them to England so soon. I will explain to them that we met with Captain Cook in the Friendly Islands, and he brought orders from the King to make another settlement in New Holland, for which they require more hogs and other livestock, and have sent us here to obtain them. You shall not tell any different story. If you do I am sure to hear of it, and you will suffer for it. You shall not mention Tubuai on pain of death. Do you all understand me?"

"Ah sure," said Byrne, "but I think I'll just get ashore and find a nice little hut and a lady to look after me, and play my fiddle in peace. What's to stop me, or any of us? I've had enough of these adventures."

Mr Christian became agitated. "Understand this," he snarled, "in the eyes of the natives this is His Majesty's Ship, and I am now its Commander. They will do for me everything they did for Bligh, and more, so if anyone chooses to desert, you will soon be brought back to me and I will not trouble to have you flogged – I'll shoot you myself! We are coming here together and we will leave together, there is no other way. You must accept that!"

Byrne's gaze was cast down as was that of the few who had nodded in agreement with him, and nothing more was said. Mr Christian had abandoned his previous character as a genial friend to all, and was now become severer, as any commander must when he wishes to impose his will on others.

Our welcome in Matavai Bay was as great as it had been before, and I had a wonderful reunion with Jenny. We still had to maintain watches, and there was much work to do in loading the ship with hogs – more than four hundred of them – as well as fifty goats, and chickens as well as cats and dogs. The natives also gave us a bull and a cow, which they did not value.

Within ten days our floating farm was ready to sail, and once again all had to bid farewell to friends and lovers. I was sorely tempted to tell Jenny of our plans, or smuggle her on board before we sailed, but I thought it better to heed Mr Christian's orders, whose aim of course was to save our necks. Others can not have been so scrupulous, because a few hours out to sea a group of natives emerged, nearly thirty in all, men, boys, women and one girl. Mr Christian was annoyed at first, but it seemed that none of these people knew our destination, so this may not have been betrayed, and they showed no dismay when he told them they would never see Otaheite again.

The seas grew rough on this crossing and the bull was severely injured and died. By some miracle nearly all the other animals survived. Once again we came to Tubuai and dropped anchor in Bloody Bay.

Our second visit to Tubuai began much better than the first. Now the natives appeared friendly, and the Chief engaged Mr Christian in much ceremony, with presents of fish, vegetables and lengths of cloth, followed by many of his people who did the same. Mr Christian presented them with knives and hatchets, as well as red feathers, and it amused us that they placed more value on the feathers, which they used for ceremonial decorations.

Now Mr Christian began to search for a place where we might live, but he found none to please him in the area where we landed, so he went to the eastern part of the island and decided on some ground there, not far from the shore. We then had to move the ship along to that part, which was not easy because of the shallows and rocks in the way, but Mr Christian sought to encourage us by saying that we would not need the ship again once we had established our dwellings ashore.

This eastern part of the island belonged to a different Chief, who gave permission to set up a camp there, but this caused jealousy in the Chief that first befriended us. The island was divided between three Chiefs, and the two whose districts we had not chosen combined against the third, and against us, refusing to supply us with any provisions, however much Mr Christian sought to reason with them. We fell to wondering whether he would ever win them round, as he planned.

Mr Christian decided to build a fort to defend our settlement, and allocated work-parties for the various tasks, including tending the live-stock, most of which were turned out on small keys (islands) off the shore. There followed many days of tree-felling for timber to make a stockade, and digging a ditch and bank on three sides facing away from the shore, each side nearly fifty yards long. All worked willingly enough, but there was also much grumbling that we had not the opportunities to consort with women that we had on Otaheite.

Although we were ordered, for the sake of discipline and security, to sleep on the ship at night, John Sumner and Matt Quintal did not come on board one evening and were away till next morning. When summoned to explain they said they were no longer ship's crew as the ship was decommissioned, so they were not obliged to be there. Christian cocked his pistol at them, swearing that he was still the master, and had them put in irons. They were released the next day after they apologised, and thereafter Mr Christian gave shore leave to two every evening, and to all on Sundays

The work continued for several weeks, and the fort, which we named 'Fort George', began to take shape. But then I became involved in an incident which led to much further trouble. On my turn ashore for the night I was walking into the woods in the hope of encountering a woman, as others boasted they had done before. Then I saw this maiden, very comely, who beckoned to me, and I followed her on a trail for some distance, into what I learned afterwards was the south-east of the island, in the third Chief's district. The witch betrayed me, for I was set upon by several men, stripped of all my clothes and imprisoned all night in a house. I do not know how Mr Christian heard of it, but the next day he led a party to the house of the Chief, who had fled. I was fetched out by the woman, though only in my shirt, to the jeers and laughter of the party. Mr Christian ordered the Chief's house set on fire, and seized some religious or ceremonial carvings, which we took away.

Some days later that Chief came to the fort and made a show of reconciliation with Mr Christian, but the natives carried concealed weapons, which we discovered, and it was certain that they meant mischief. Mr Christian declined to sit down and drink yava, so the Chief stamped away in anger. His men produced their weapons and threatened to invade us, but one shot from a cannon dispersed them.

"Well, Alex," said Ned, "you have lost your breeches and we have gained no friends from your night ashore. I wonder if we will ever be at peace here."

There never was any peace on Tubuai. This was not just because of our troubles with the natives, but we also started quarrels amongst ourselves, and with Mr Christian. Quintal, McCoy, Sumner, Martin and others whose loyalty he had never had reason to doubt complained to him that they could get no women, because the Chiefs would not let them come to us on the ship.

"Well, you can make free with them ashore," was Christian's response.

"Aye, and look what happened to Alex," said Quintal, "we have no security there at night. How long before one of us is knocked on the head?"

"We can not go on like this!" shouted Isaac Martin, "We took the ship for you and now all we have is digging a ditch and stoning by savages."

"Mr Christian, if the Chiefs will not let the women come to us, let us simply go and take them!" cried Quintal.

Others roared their approval of this suggestion. Christian was aghast.

"So you may spend a few nights in fornication and the rest of your days avoiding stones and spears," he said. "We can do no such thing as you suggest. I will not hear of it again."

"Then we will work no more," was the cry.

For three days this argument raged. I felt no strong support for Quintal and the others because I did not believe that taking a woman by force would yield a happy union, but I shared the dismay of all that our life there promised none of the tranquil bliss that we had enjoyed on Otaheite. In their idleness men took to drink, and when Mr Christian refused to increase the grog ration they broke into the store and took it anyway, so he doubled the ration, but it made no difference. The ship was in ferment, all now seemed as unhappy as ever they had been under Captain Bligh.

Work on the fort had stopped, as had the supply the supply of produce from the natives, so Mr Christian called all together to discuss how we might proceed.

"It will soon be three months since we came here this time, said Jim Morrison, "and we are still living like rats on this accursed ship."

"Aye, and nearly five months since you and your villains took the ship, Christian," chimed in Byrne, as he always did, "and we have nothing to show for it, not even our miserable pay. If you had not turned out Captain Bligh we might now be nearly at the West Indies."

"And if you played the fiddle better you might be leading an orchestra," snarled Churchill. "We are here together and can only subdue those savages if we work together."

"We will never be safe here," shouted Mr Coleman the Armourer, "we should return to Otaheite where we know we will be welcomed."

"Nay, we shall not, and you know my reasons for that," retorted Christian.

"Why should we not take the ship to Otaheite, and you, and any as want to, remain here?" cried someone. Mr Christian scowled, and in a rage drew the pistol that he always carried.

"Understand this! None of you will take this ship from me. You may depend on that."

With that he turned away abruptly and went to his cabin, leaving us to argue without any outcome. Later that evening Ned Young knocked on his door and spent a long time in conversation with him. Afterwards he told me that Christian had agreed to allow a vote on returning to Otaheite, as there would be little he could do to prevent that if it was the will of the majority.

The next day, sixteen hands showed in favour of return, and it was then agreed that those who stayed in Otaheite should have their share of weapons and other items, but Mr Christian would remain in control of the ship and go wherever he chose afterwards. Now, there was much bustle and preparation to ready the ship for sea again, though only a few days before Mr Christian had been talking about taking out the masts for use in the fort. Also, a party was sent out to recover some of the live-stock that had been let loose ashore – and this led to our final unhappy dealings with this island.

Twenty of us set out, with nine of the Otaheitean men, to find the hogs and cow which were mostly held in the district where I was taken prisoner. We had to pass through the wood, where we were set upon by a large number of natives wielding clubs and spears, and hurling stones. Tom Burkitt took a spear in his side, then we loosed a musket volley which felled a good number. Our Otaheitean friends took up the spears of those who had fallen, and bravely fought alongside us as we faced several more attacks and shot many of them. Only after a Chief was shot dead did they back away and harry us no more. Burkitt was not severely hurt, and we collected what animals we could, returning them to the ship.

We sailed about three days after that, having been joined by a young Chief who had befriended Mr Christian, with two of his friends. His name was Taroamiva, and he wished to leave Tubuai because he feared being killed if he remained. He said that sixty of the other tribe had been killed in that battle.

"Well, we've left them a fair few hogs, as well as cats and dogs, and a fine ditch," said Ned, as the ship cleared the reef and set a course for Otaheite.

"Aye, it'll serve to bury their dead," said Byrne.

Michael Byrne never failed to decry anyone's deeds or to dampen their spirits, which is why he was disliked by all, but this time he was perfectly justified in what he said. We had come to Tubuai and completely disturbed the lives of all who lived there, because we assumed we should have the right to settle there. Now sixty had been killed in one day, and others before then, and they would be alive if we had not gone there.

The dream that there was some new Paradise waiting to welcome us died on Tubuai, along with most of Fletcher Christian's authority.

Chapter 13 – Voyage to Pitcairn

On that last voyage to Otaheite the stores were divided so that the sixteen men going ashore should easily take what was due to them. We anchored again in Matavai Bay, and the "deserters", as Quintal called them, busied themselves in landing everything they needed for their life there, however long that might be. During the day, some native men and women came on board, including Christian's sweetheart, that he called 'Mainmast' because she was so tall, and my own Jenny, who I was delighted to see. However, we noticed that no Chief came out to welcome us, and after Ned mentioned this to Mr Christian, he became more anxious, and cast many glances at the shore throughout that afternoon.

All of us who wished to sail on did not go ashore that day, and Mr Christian told Morrison and the other "deserters" that we would stay a day or two, that we might take on water and all might ensure that there had been a fair division of all the goods. However, before darkness fell he summoned us to a meeting, that is the eight who had voted not to stay at Otaheite – Ned Young, John Williams, Will McCoy, Matt Quintal, Isaac Martin, Jack Mills, Billy Brown and me.

"Shipmates, as long as we stay here, we are not safe. I believe Morrison and some of the others might try to take the ship from us, and have the help of Tynah or some other Chief, because none has come to greet us. We must leave immediately."

"And our visitors?" asked Ned.

"Batten them below, until we are out to sea. We should not be without our women. Now, Billy, take an axe to the anchor cable, Alex and Jack set the fore staysail to swing her head round seawards. Ned, take the wheel, and the rest of you ready to set the fore and main topsails when she comes round."

As we went to our tasks we heard a shout, and I saw Mr Coleman the Armourer shaking his fist at Mr Christian. We had not realised that he was still on board, doubtless he had been seeking some more ironware to take ashore.

"Kidnap me will you, damn your eyes!" he shouted.

"Be easy, John, we did not intend it, but we're under way now, there's no going back, and we'll be glad of your skills."

"Be damned to that, I've had no part in your piracy, and will not join it now!" And with that, Coleman jumped over the side and swam away.

As we went out through the reef and allowed our 'visitors' on deck, so that they saw our intention, they were somewhat agitated, and one woman followed Coleman by jumping overboard, though she had much further to swim. In the following days there was much argument by some of the women, even Jenny cried a little, and there arose a coolness between us which never really went away after that. Six of the women were quite old, and they made the most noise, so that for the sake of peace Mr Christian had us launch a boat and put them ashore on an island that we passed, hoping that they would have a chance to get back to Otaheite. They seemed happy to go on that island, but I sometimes wonder whether they did go back to Otaheite, or how long their welcome by the people there would have lasted if they did not. After that, Mr Christian was careful not to sail too close to any island in case more were tempted to swim away, but after a time everyone settled down and lived on board in harmony.

So it was that with the nine of us who sailed away from Otaheite there were six men. Three of them were the young Chief from Tubuai and his two servants – that is Taroamiva (who changed his name to Tetahiti when we came to Pitcairn) with Teimua and

Oha. They were greatly impressed by Mr Christian and happy to sail anywhere with him. The other three were from Otaheite, named Menari, Tararoa and Nihu. They also seemed content to stay on board with us.

There remained eleven women, and mostly we gave them English names, so I do not trouble with their native ones. As well as Mainmast and Jenny there were Nancy, Susan, Sarah and Prudence. One I call Tina, though her Otaheitean name was longer than that, and Mareva, Obuarei, Faahotu and Teio, who I was married to under English law much later, by Captain Beechey, though she was first McCoy's woman. Indeed, there were many different unions between those who first came to Pitcairn.

It was not so easy to sail the ship now that there were only nine of us who were sailors, and we durst not carry too much sail, particularly at night, for fear we might be overpowered by squalls. Because of that our progress was slow, also because the hull was becoming fouled, as there had been no cleaning of it since long before the mutiny. Before long we had the assistance of the native men who became adept at climbing the rigging and working aloft once we showed them what to do, which relieved our burden. However, because they were following our commands, and we became used to giving them, they were always treated as inferiors, which led to strife later on.

At first Mr Christian took us westward towards the Friendly Islands where we had mutinied. When we left Otaheite he said there was a group of islands which had been found by the Spanish, where we might find a safe haven, but we passed some weeks scouting round islands which were either too small to offer a safe haven or were populated by natives who seemed hostile. No-one wished to repeat the experience we had on Tubuai, and we demanded that Mr Christian should find us a safe berth elsewhere, or we would go back to Otaheite and take our chance with the others.

Mr Christian spent many hours studying the charts and reading almanacks and accounts by Captain Cook and others of the islands of the Pacific Ocean. Finally he came to us and told us of an island called Pitcairn, which was more than two thousand miles to the east of where we were. This had been sighted by a British ship some twenty years before but no landing had ever been recorded, and it was thought to be uninhabited. Quintal expressed the doubt that was in the minds of us all;

"So what shall we do if we sail two thousand miles and find another hell-hole like Tubuai? Otaheite seems as if it is the only safe place where we will have a welcome."

"We have food and water enough to make the passage," said Christian, "and then to go back to Otaheite, or to try for the Marquesas Islands, which are to the north of Pitcairn and no further than Oatheite from there."

In a spirit of resignation and hope we agreed with Mr Christian's proposal. He now could lead us only by persuasion, but we felt we had not much choice but to go along with him for the time being at least. We tracked across that empty ocean, leaving Otaheite and Tubuai a long way to the north, for two months or more, but when we were told to look out for the island, it was not there.

Now angry voices were raised, Quintal and McCoy in particular, while Christian could find little to say, and looked downcast. It was Ned who took control.

"Fletcher, we are where the chart says, at twenty-five degrees two minutes south, and we have been sailing due east for some days, so there is nothing west of here on this latitude, do you agree?"

Christian nodded.

"We know it is not difficult for any navigator to fix a latitude, but in the past it was never easy to calculate the longitude accurately without a good chronometer – so perhaps the original sighting was east of here and wrongly recorded."

"That's it!" Christian jumped to his feet, the light returning to his eyes. "Men, it was a British vessel which sighted Pitcairn, so we need have little doubt that it is there somewhere. As Ned says, the position on the chart may be a mistake many navigators have made. We shall sail in shallow tacks either side of twenty-five degrees south, but heave to at night so that we do not miss it, and I'll lay we find Pitcairn in five days. And when we do it will be a long time before anyone finds us, because the chart will lie to them as well."

"Five days it is then, Christian," growled Quintal to murmurs of assent, "else you'll be in a boat and I'll be shouting 'Huzzah for Otaheite' again."

On the fifth evening we sighted Pitcairn. At the midday following we came up to the island on its southern side, viewing it both with excitement and concern, as the ocean swell beat against almost sheer cliffs without the protection of a reef, and it seemed impossible to land anywhere along there. Above those cliffs the land rose up to a mountain range, but on the slopes were trees and vegetation of all kinds, and Billy Brown remarked that the soil must be fertile. We saw no signs of life.

On we sailed and soon came to a headland at the eastern end, where we tacked and made a course westward along the northern shore. Here also the cliffs were steep, but we spied a broad bay which could afford shelter from winds from some quarters. We sailed on, along the remainder of the northern coast up to the western headland, but saw no other inlet more promising than the bay we had seen before. We hove to a few miles off for the night, and did not see any fires or other lights ashore. The next day we returned to the place we now call 'Bounty Bay', which is still the only place where a safe landing can be made on Pitcairn, and then not for landlubbers or the faint-hearted. Even then the wind was from the north, and we could see that the surf was very rough, so we did not care to risk our boat or ourselves on an unknown shore. We stood off for another two days before the wind veered easterly, and the waves became less violent. Then, with just staysail and mizzen we approached and dropped anchor about two hundred yards off shore. Mr Christian asked, rather than ordered, Ned, Jack Mills, John Williams and me to remain with the ship, and Quintal, McCoy, Martin and Billy Brown to go ashore with him in the boat, also Tetahiti and Menari. I am sure he chose us to remain because he trusted us not to sail away, while Quintal and McCoy might have betrayed him if he had left them on board.

They were gone above three hours. When they returned, Mr Christian had a joyful expression such as we had not seen on him for a long time past, and the others, too, were excited and jovial.

"Shipmates, we will be shipmates no more, but neighbours and farmers!" exclaimed Christian. "It's a steep way up, but there's a large piece of ground above where we can live, enough for us all, and the whole place is deserted. We have no natives to worry us this time!"

"Yes, I have already seen breadfruit, coconuts and plantains, and fresh water streams, so with the live-stock and seeds that we have, we can live here as easily as we could on Otaheite," said Billy.

"And what think you, Matt?" asked Ned, "Is it still 'Hurrah for Otaheite'?"

"I suppose this will do," grunted Quintal with a shrug.

"Matt, we could not find anywhere better!" cried Christian, once again the cheerful and friendly Lieutenant that we had seen on the 'Bounty' before his troubles with Captain Bligh. "As Billy has said, we have the land and the means to maintain ourselves here, we have our women, there is little more we could expect elsewhere in the whole of the Pacific. And never forget, as I told you before, the Navy will come and find those who stayed on Otaheite – but the only chart where Pitcairn is marked shows it one hundred and eighty miles west of here. It may be that no-one will find us in our lifetime!"

That became true for all on board except me and most of the women, but I do not suppose that when Christian said it, he expected his, and the others', lives to be so short.

There was a commotion amongst the natives, who had been standing apart and addressed by Tetahiti and Menari. There was cheering, and some of the women began to dance a heiva.

"The island pleases them, it would seem, said Ned.

"Och, Tetahiti found some symbols carved on a rock face," said McCoy. "They must be from people that lived here before, because there is no sign of life now. They seem to think it is a good omen."

"Indeed, it must be!" cried Christian, "let's drink to that!" We drank heartily, and no useful work was done during the remainder of that day. A spirit of comradeship and well-being pervaded all, but maybe that was the last time that every person felt such goodwill,as, once ashore, the quarrels were not long in starting.

Mr Christian's last entry in the log he kept, which I still have, is dated 15th January 1790 - "Pitcairn(?) sighted." After that, it seems his only thought was of leaving the ship and becoming a farmer.

Chapter 14 – The end of the 'Bounty'

The next morning we came together again on deck. Mr Christian still addressed us as our leader.

"Today we should make a camp, use some of the sails for shelter, take the weapons and enough food for several days, and make sure of a supply of water. Once all are safe ashore, we must then dispose of the ship."

"How so, dispose of the ship?" asked Billy Brown.

"Billy, there is no safe anchorage here, and sooner or later she will be carried away in a storm. Also, if she is sighted by passing vessels, they would likely send a party to investigate, and we will be discovered. When we are ready we will drive her ashore, and take away as much as we can. There is enough timber in her to build us all fine houses."

We went ashore that day and felled timber for poles to make our shelter. Much of the stores we ferried ashore on a raft, which we attached on a line to a buoy anchored fifty yards off the beach beyond the line of the surf so that we could more easily get away from the beach every time. But everything we sent that way got a fair wetting, and we soon tired of it. The time had come for the 'Bounty's final short voyage.

Mr Christian himself took the wheel, and under staysails and mizzen alone he steered the ship slowly towards the cove, where Mills and Martin were waiting with a line fastened round a large jutting rock. Quintal and I were at the bow, with lines readied to cast ashore. The rollers picked up the ship as she approached and Mr Christian fought with the wheel as he sought to prevent her broaching and being rolled over. With a final surge as the waves broke under her and crashed against the stern, there was an almighty jolt as she struck and came to rest less than a ship's length from the beach. Mr Christian was flung to the deck and we lost our footing, but quickly recovered and threw our lines to the beach party, who secured them to theirs so that the ship remained where she was.

We rigged a cable and blocks to send everything ashore, and let the live-stock down so that they could swim for it, which they did well. We lost none to the waves, but a number of the goats escaped up the cliffs and ran wild, so that you see their descendants on the hillside today. The fowls were penned up and winched ashore in perfect safety.

We toiled for three days, unloading everything that was moveable and stripping out some timber, including some of the spars. The hardest task was not taking it from the ship, but carrying it up to our camp, because the path was very steep and difficult, as it still is, although we have made it wider and a little easier since then.

There was still a great deal of timber that we could have used if we had cut it out, and Mr Christian was talking of taking out the masts. However, late on the third afternoon as we wearily hauled our burdens up to the camp and looked back down at the bay, we saw a thick column of smoke.

"My God, what are they doing?" exclaimed Christian, and began to run down the hill, as we followed. On the 'Bounty's foredeck Quintal and McCoy were dancing a jig, laughing and singing, and so drunk they could hardly keep their feet.

"I thought we had taken all the grog and spirits ashore already," said Christian in exasperation.

"They must have found some more," I said.

From the hatchways thick smoke and flames were pouring, and the ship was obviously well ablaze.

"Damn you!" shouted Mr Christian, "we need that timber, what possessed you to burn it?"

"Och away," spluttered McCoy, "we've enough already, I'm tired of scrambling up yon cliff like a goat."

"I should decide when we have timber enough," shouted Christian, "not you!"

"Is that so?" laughed Quintal. "You were elected Captain for the voyage, but that is over. Now we're landlubbers, and I'll not have you as my lord and master."

Mr Christian turned away in despair. The flames burst through the quarterdeck and the two drunks hastily climbed down a rope and stumbled ashore through the surf.

"Matt, you're a fool," I said.

"Maybe, but I've had a bellyful of tugging my forelock to officers who think that the sun shines out of their arses. From now on I'll do things as I please and in my own time."

"This island is not so big that we can live apart and take no heed of each other. You may not care for Christian or accept his authority, but if we can not all agree to work together we will have a hard time of it here."

He looked at me with bloodshot eyes, as dull and uncomprehending as one of the pigs that we had lately herded up the cliff. Drunk or sober, Matt Quintal was 'born to trouble', as the prayer-book says. As the sparks flew upwards from the inferno of the 'Bounty', I turned to the path and left him beside his companion, who was now lying on the stones just above the tide, and snoring loudly.

The following morning all that was left of the ship was a mess of wreckage in the surf. The hull had burned down to the waterline and the remainder had sunk. We retrieved some parts of the masts and spars that had fallen clear, and left the rest to be devoured by the sea.

"Well, Quintal has ensured that Christian may not take us anywhere else."

"Be damned to that, her back was broken, the keel timber cracked when he drove her ashore."

"Maybe, but we could have saved much more of her. Now we have to get what we can from this wilderness."

Such was the conversation as some of us looked down at those mournful remnants in the bay. Now we had fulfilled Mr Christian's dream of finding a place to settle where no-one would find us, but I believe many had the same thoughts as I, that we might spend the rest of our lives without seeing another human face except those around us now, never sit down in a friendly tavern or stroll around a busy market-place. Now it had come to us, the thought of being so cut off from the rest of the world was oppressive. Taking the ship had felt like a fine adventure, but now the ship, our last link with the outside world, was gone.

It was Billy Brown who brought us back to the moment.

"We should not delay in breaking ground to sow some of the seed we have, yams, corn and the like."

"Quite so, said Mr Christian, who had approached just then, "there is much to do. We can mark out our fields for each of us this very day."

"You would not make a farm common to all of us?" asked Ned.

"I think not, let each profit by his own labours, and there is enough land for nine of us."

I imagine Mr Christian proposed separate enterprise because he no longer had need of us, and the only one who could aspire to be close to his social equal was Ned Young. However, we did not disagree with his proposal, for none could be confident in any undertaking in common with the likes of McCoy and Quintal. And, Heaven be praised, we were to become what we never could in England, we were landowners!

"What of Tetahiti and the others, should they not also have their patch?" asked Jack Mills.

"Good Lord, no, the natives are no farmers!" Christian exclaimed. I thought that with the exception of Billy Brown, neither were we, but remained silent. "They will help us in our labours, and we can share the fruits thereof with them. I will explain all to Tetahiti."

The rest of that day we spent in marking out the places where we were to build our houses, around a central green like an English village, then tramping over the island with the 'Bounty's lead-line for a measure, so that no man should have an unequal share. It did not occur to any of us that it was unfair not to award allotments to the native men too, but as I said before, on Otaheite we were treated as a superior race, on the ship we were naturally the masters, and when we came ashore we did not feel any differently. Thus they became our servants, as the women were already our concubines, and as I look back I can not deny that this caused the troubles that led to the deaths of all those native men and most of the nine of us who paced out our land that day.

Many days of toil ensued, as we turned over the soil to prepare for planting, and erected the frames of our houses. Many a curse was uttered in the direction of McCoy and Quintal as we sweated at felling timber and sawing planks, as we might have saved some of that labour but for their foolhardy drunkenness. The native men all willingly shared the burden, being at that time volunteers rather than the pressed men they later became. The women, too, were eager to help in the fields and tend the animals, and it was not long before they sought out the plants and trees from which, in Otaheite and the other Pacific islands that I saw, the bark is taken and beaten out to make cloth, which can be as fine as the product of any loom. Cloth was always an important matter to all the Pacific peoples, presented as a gift or used at ceremonies, and our women were not long in establishing such a craft on Pitcairn.

I have said "our women", and I can only say with sorrow that in those early years here they were our chattels, and often not well used. It was one of the first quarrels that we had with the natives, because we all took women and between six of them they had but three women, while Tetahiti, who had been a chief would not share, and the women did not like two of the men, who were forced to live the life of monks. While these women were with their native men they never produced any offspring, and the only children born here are descended from 'Bounty' mutineers.

It is also with sorrow that I remember how the love Jenny and I had for each other died. She never forgave me for taking her away from Otaheite, and became sullen in my presence, and unresponsive when I kissed her. At that time I had learned very little of the Otaheitean tongue, indeed I still know little, so I could not reason with her. She went to stay with Isaac Martin, and I let her go. I believe she truly loved me on Otaheite, but her heart always remained there, and she went back there a few years ago, the only one of those who came on the 'Bounty' to do so.

For a while I took no special "wife", though I would become the husband of several later on. Sarah, though she bore him several children, was cruelly treated by Quintal, and Teio was made miserable by McCoy, so that she often came to me for comfort when he was drunk, and then stayed with me later on when he went.

Chapter 15 – Pitcairn in turmoil

Ten months after our arrival, Mainmast bore the first of our children. Christian named the boy Thursday October, those being the day and month of his birth. Ned asked him why he had not chosen a normal English Christian name such as we all had, and he muttered only that he did not care for such names. I can only take that as a sign of the madness that was now descending on his soul. How can anyone who cared for their child give them such a name? He might as well have given him a number. He did not show that he disliked the boy, but I think he did not love him either, indeed there was little sign that he still loved anything about his life. He ignored us all, and even Ned, to whom he still spoke sometimes, grew tired of his sullen moods. True, he still worked on his field and on building a more permanent house than the first rude shelters that we made, but he never sought our assistance, although we often helped each other. Instead he called on the native men and berated them like the meanest servants when they failed to do what he expected. Sometimes his rages sounded like those of Captain Bligh.

After some time we noticed that he disappeared for long periods, but one day Martin and Mills followed him and discovered his secret. In a rock-face high on the mountain-side is a cave hidden from below by trees and accessible only along a narrow and dangerous ledge. When the two men approached, Christian waved a pistol at them.

"Keep back! Why do you come to spy on me?"

"Peace, we are unarmed," said Jack, "we come not to spy, but from concern for your well-being. If you become unwell, or are injured, how can we help you if no-one knows where you are?"

Christian allowed them to come further, and inside the cave they saw crude bedding made from palm and plantain leaves, as well as food and two muskets.

"Here I have a clear view of the bay and the path up to the camp," said Christian. "If they come for me I have time to prepare, and can sell my life dearly. But I will share it with nobody, this is my retreat alone."

Poor Fletcher Christian! In the few years before his death he spent much of his time in that cave, with only his demons for company. The debonair Lieutenant, the most popular man on the 'Bounty' had now become a brooding monster, hated by all the Indians, shunning and shunned by all of us. He despised the society of those who had supported him all the way to find exactly the refuge he sought, but his refuge was now a prison. He faced a lifetime barred from the society where he had once aspired to flourish. Not for him the genteel soirées, the balls, the card tables or witty coffee-house discourse! Now he must till the soil and endure the ill-educated chatter of common sailors for ever.

"Sell his life dearly, will he?" laughed Quintal after Martin and Mills recounted their visit to Christian's cave. "If the Navy hoisted a cannon up from the beach his life wouldn't be worth much."

Sunday worship is now the foundation of our lives here, but it had been largely forgotten after we took the 'Bounty'. Mr Christian made an attempt to restore this mark of civilisation, but had little support from most of us, and his heart was not in it as he surrendered his soul to the devil, as I believe he did, and he gave it up. But it was those few occasions when he read from the Bible that I wished I could read those stories for myself, and said as much to Ned. He said there was no reason why I should not if I would undertake the labour of learning to read. I have found it as hard as any other labour I have done on Pitcairn, and

I still only read slowly, but well enough. The labour of writing, however, is still beyond me for the most part. Nevertheless, the beginning that I made with Ned allowed me, after all the disasters that were to come, when I was the only man left alive, to guide our community into a life of peace and righteousness.

The first of these disasters befell us not long after Thursday October was born, when we lost two of the women. Faahotu was taken sick and died, and Obuarei, the wife of John Williams, fell down a cliff when she was collecting birds' eggs, and was killed. John Williams was always a steadfast man who loyally supported Mr Christian during the mutiny and afterwards. He had been the Armourer's mate on the 'Bounty', and his skills as a blacksmith were much prized by us after Coleman had jumped overboard when we left Otaheite. He had set up a forge by the village and was happy with his lot until he lost Obuarei, but after that he became restive.

"I can bear this no more," he said one evening when all of us, even Christian, were gathered in fellowship. "I think I will leave this island."

"How can you leave?" I asked.

"We still have the two boats from the 'Bounty'. I can make one fit for a voyage back to Otaheite."

"That is more than one thousand miles from here, and you have not the skills of a navigator," said Mr Christian. "It is your skills at the forge that we need here. And what ails you so much that you must leave us?"

"I can not live the rest of my life as a monk, while all of you have women."

"Is that all?" laughed Quintal. "Why, that is easily remedied – take a wife from the natives."

"Oh, I think that was what you proposed on Tubuai," said Ned doubtfully.

"Aye, but there we had a whole tribe to fight. Here there are but six of them, and we are their masters."

There were some sympathetic murmurs at this, and Mr Christian sat in silent thought for a few moments.

"Well, John, if we arrange a wife for you, shall we have no more talk of going away in a boat, where you will certainly perish?"

"I would be beholden to you, Mr Christian, as always," replied Williams.

So it was that the following afternoon Williams and I went to find Nancy, as she became known, and Tina where they were working and led them away to our houses with little explanation, Williams taking Nancy, and I Tina. They came willingly enough. They came willingly enough, I think because they should no longer be looked down on by the other women who were already the wives of white men.

At the same time Mr Christian, accompanied by Quintal and Martin, all armed, went to tell Tetahiti and his companions what was being done, and they must all henceforth be content with just one woman, Mareva. Even from the distance where they were, in my house we could hear the shouts of rage. As she lay beside me Tina smiled at me and uttered soothing words as she stroked my cheek.

In the following weeks the native men showed their displeasure by refusing to work in the fields, and Williams and I in particular received many dark looks from them, and were careful never to be alone in their company. It was still a shock when we realised that Tetahiti, Teimua and Oha were planning to kill us all.

One evening we were gathered in conversation while the women nearby sat around a fire and sang, as they often did. Suddenly Ned turned his head and raised his hand;

"Hush, hark at those women, what are they singing?" He understood their language better than most of us, and he exclaimed,

"Aye, there it is again! 'Why does black man sharpen axe – to kill white man'!"

As they sang this, several of the women were looking towards us, so that we should be in no doubt of their message. Ned went over to them and after a few moments' conversation came back, and told us of the plot by those three.

Although Mr Christian by now wielded little authority over us, he still had much more with the natives. He sought out Tetahiti and told him that we knew of the plot; we could not continue in daily fear of our lives, and if the natives would not work then we might as well kill them all. However, Tetahiti, albeit one of the conspirators, could be spared if he and the three who had not conspired would do away with Teimua and Oha. Those two soon learned their fate and fled into the woods, but were pursued by the other four and clubbed to death. And so we brought murder to Pitcairn. I had no direct hand in it, but I felt a deep unease because I had been running away from such evil all my life, and there seemed no refuge from it.

In the next year one further child was born, that was Matthew Quintal, named after his father, and the year after that came four more, Charles Christian, named, I believe after Fletcher Christian's brother, then Elizabeth Mills, Daniel McCoy and John Quintal, although he did not live long. Mary Ann Christian and John Mills, also named after his father, came in the third year, but that was another bloodstained year in the short history of this island.

I thank God that those children and the others who came after know little of those dark times, and that He in His mercy has not visited on them the sins of their fathers. After the murder of their two compatriots the remaining native men found themselves in a life of servitude to us with only Mareva to console them, which caused them many disagreements, but also, I am sure, increased their hatred of us.

I did not quarrel too badly with any of them, and found them willing helpers when they were rewarded with a little extra food. I was the only one of us who went fishing with them, because I had grown up in that trade, and I suppose they might have easily drowned me if they wished, but they did not. Ned, too, treated them well so had few quarrels with them, also because he spoke their tongue well enough. However, Isaac Martin, who had not even restrained himself from beating a native on Otaheite, and been flogged for it, was now quite free with his fists and boots. Quintal and McCoy, too, who themselves had endured a life close to the gutter, now took pleasure in ill-treating those they perceived to be lower than themselves. One day McCoy ordered Teimua to hoe his field, but did not go with him, instead returning to his house to sleep. Teimua hoed only a few yards, then went away. When McCoy found how little he had done, he chased him into the woods and beat him severely. John Williams, who caused the first revolt when the two women were taken away, kept away from the natives, and for a long time carried a weapon wherever he went, in his forge or in his field.

Fletcher Christian was by now completely changed from the amiable character he once had been into a morose monster, as liable to snarl at his former shipmates as at the natives. I saw him one day, cutlass in hand forcing Tetahiti to kneel before him and berating him because of something he had failed to do. This was Tetahiti, once his friend and formerly a Chief of some sort amongst his people on Tubuai, forced to grovel in the dirt. How foolish it was to believe that such treatment could go on without retribution!

The retribution, when it came, was swift and terrible, and whether or not they knew of it, we had no warning from the women this time. Several of us were working alone on our fields that morning, and as I dug up some yams I heard a shot from the direction of the village. I thought little of it, as it was not unusual for any of us to pick off some of the hogs and goats that had run wild after getting ashore from the 'Bounty', and they or their offspring would come down and root in our plantations. McCoy and Quintal, particularly, preferred this sport to the labour of tending their fields. But this was not they, I do not know how Tetahiti and his band obtained their firearms, but they had them, and the shot I heard, as I learned later, had killed John Williams in his forge.

I then heard another shot and a cry from Christian's field, which was separated from mine by a small wood. I started towards it just as Tetahiti and his three followers, armed with muskets and mattocks, emerged from the thicket. I turned and ran, but heard a shot and felt a terrible pain at the base of my neck which fired through my brain and I fell down unconscious. I may not have been senseless for very long, but I lay for some minutes in case they were still nearby. I heard only two more shots further away, and then silence for a while. They must have thought me dead, or else in their haste to pursue the others had not troubled to despatch me. Now I heard women wailing, and some came and helped me into Christian's house, where they dressed my wound. The bullet had not penetrated far so that they were able to cut it out, though that was very painful for a time.

As I rested, Ned came in and told what had happened. He was about the village when he saw them go in and shoot Williams, so he had hastened to hide with the women, who like him and were happy to save him. The men had then gone after Christian, who was now dead, then they had shot Jack Mills, who thought they were only seeking McCoy and Quintal, and stood to parley with them. Finally they came up with Isaac Martin, whom they clubbed to death, and Billy Brown, who was shot – poor Billy, who never hurt a fly, and helped us so much with our farming!

"And Quintal and McCoy?" I asked.

"Aye, there's the rub," said Ned, "I imagine they wanted to kill those two more than any of us, but they got out of the village and escaped up the mountain. Maybe they're up at Christian's cave, or have gone round the southern side of the mountain, who can tell?"

"So now we are four, as are they."

"That is so, and we have to find some way to live together, but that may not be easy. If Tetahiti goes hunting for those two he may decide to finish us off as well. I will need to reason with him – but later, 'sufficient unto the day is the evil thereof', as the Gospel tells us. Rest and regain your strength, Alex."

My shoulder healed gradually, but the wounds in our community festered and grew poisonous. Now the four natives took the upper hand, and I was too weak to oppose them. Ned was able to maintain an uneasy truce, and it was fortunate that Quintal and McCoy did not attempt to return just then. Tetahiti and his men no longer seemed so troubled by those two as to wish to hunt them down, instead their sole desire was to possess women who had been denied to them for so long.

This sudden power fired their minds and turned them into lustful ravening beasts, so that they seized any woman at will, even taking away Nancy and Tina who afterwards returned sobbing to my house. During that reign of terror I slept with a pistol and cutlass by our bed, and ventured out little, and never unarmed. Our fields went mostly untended.

This state of affairs did not last long because in their madness the natives began to quarrel with each other. One evening I heard a shot, and seizing my weapons I peered cautiously out from my door. Jenny came running out of Isaac Martin's house, which she and the natives were using, and I beckoned her indoors.

"Menari shoot Teimua!" As best I could understand they had been arguing over Sarah and Teio, and Menari had resolved the matter by force.

Menari also met his end soon after, though this was at the hands of Quintal and McCoy, as they told us afterwards. They had been lurking on the outskirts of the village for some days, awaiting opportunities to steal more food for themselves, and had come upon Menari when he went to a stream to bathe, so they shot him.

Now that there remained only Tetahiti and Nihu, their power over us drained away. The women, too, were emboldened to resist their advances, and one night Tetahiti was poisoned by Susan, who had been a favourite of Ned. The remaining poor brute had not the sense to moderate his behaviour, and when Ned heard Nancy screaming as Nihu forced himself on her, he knocked him down with a pistol butt and then shot him dead.

Thus ended those men from Tubuai and Otaheite whom we had brought to Pitcairn. We brought them, so although they murdered many of us, and might have ended by killing all of us, God may judge ours as the greater responsibility, and the greater crime.

I confess also that the demise of those men did not bring peace to our island, as Ned and I hoped, and as it should have done. Quintal and McCoy returned to us, but their behaviour now was worse than ever it was before, and they would not in any way be constrained to observe the decencies required to live in harmony with others. They both treated their wives terribly, and it was a miracle that Sarah gave Quintal another four children over the next few years. McCoy managed to father but one more girl, Catherine, by Teio, before he destroyed himself.

In the year following that massacre Ned became a proud father for the first time when Nancy gave him a pretty daughter, Polly. But that was a rare happy event in a time of great unease, particularly amongst the women, who had been so roughly used, not only by the native men, but by some of us as well. Ned came to me one day and said;

"Did you know that our shipmates were not buried, as we thought? The women would not do it! I have just found Jenny handling a skull, which she said was John Williams. They have the others, too. She said that there is a great hole in Fletcher

Christian's skull where Tetahiti hit him with an axe after they shot him."

"But why would they keep such trophies? Is this some witchcraft?"

"I do not know. I told her they must give up these remains for a decent burial, else we will force them, but she will not, and I do not know where they are hidden."

A day later he spoke to me again.

"Jenny said that she and some of the others are bitterly unhappy and want us to give them a boat so that they can leave this island."

"Leave! It made no sense for John Williams to try, so they are unlikely to fare better, and we should not give up our boat."

"She said that if we give them a boat they will surrender the remains of their shipmates when they go. I agree we should not give up our boat, but what if we build one for them?"

For the sake of peace I agreed but Quintal and McCoy complained long and loudly, as two of the women most anxious to leave were Teio and Sarah. Their complaints were ignored and we started work down at the cove. In her eagerness to assist, Jenny tore down some of the timber off her house, planking which had originally been taken off the 'Bounty'.

"So the old ship goes back to sea," laughed Ned, "I've told Jenny to keep a good watch over it, lest Quintal sets it ablaze."

In little more than a week it was finished.

"We are little use as carpenters, it looks ungainly to my eye," I said.

"It might not pass an Admiralty inspection, but I am sure it will float," said Ned.

We loaded on as much in the way of supplies as the boat would hold, and six of them, Jenny, Teio, Sarah, Susan, Mareva and

Prudence pushed off through the surf, shipping a lot of water, and pulled on their oars. It was a fine day when they set off, but they had gone little more than half a mile when a sudden squall, such as is common on this ocean, overtook them, and the boat foundered, waterlogged as it was already. They all managed to swim back to the shore. It is a mercy that they had progressed no further, as the same disaster must have overtaken them sooner or later when they had no shore to swim to.

We showed, and indeed felt, no triumph at their failure, and helped them back up the path to the village. That evening I could hear once again the angry shouts of Quintal, and Sarah sobbing. The following day we laid to rest in a common grave the bones of Fletcher Christian, John Williams, John Mills, Isaac Martin and William Brown.

Chapter 16 – Sole Survivor

Our troubles with the women were not yet over because a few months later, Quintal told us that Sarah and some others were planning to kill us all. We could understand why she would want to be rid of him, but at first did not believe they would want to punish us as well. However, Ned asked Mainmast, who had sought solace in his arms since Christian's death, and she confessed that there had been wild talk of murdering us all in our beds because, as they thought, we white men were possessed by some evil spirit which would lead us to kill all of their kind.

We gathered everyone together, and Ned told the women that we possessed no evil spirits, and had no thought of harming them. We were sorry that the native men had been killed, but the cause of the quarrel with them no longer existed, and the women's lives would be better with our labour to provide for them, and the children would have fathers. We did not wish to punish them, which we must if they would not live in peace with us. Their eyes downcast, they nodded their heads and went away.

After that we settled down to live as I imagine any small village in England must do. We improved our houses, we tended our crops and caught our fish by net and line. The first babies were now starting to walk and talk, and more came, two for Quintal by Sarah, and Mainmast gave a son, Edward, to Ned. In that same year Dinah was my first-born, her mother being Prudence. The following year Ned fathered two more, Dorothy by Mainmast, and George by Nancy. Prudence gave me Rachel, and Sarah gave her name to another daughter of Quintal.

Mr Christian's confidence in the remoteness of Pitcairn as a hiding-place was well justified, as during those early years we only sighted two ships that I can remember, a great distance off, and I suppose they had little curiosity about an island in a place not marked on their charts. I had a strange feeling when I saw them, because, though I did not wish to be discovered, I would have liked once again to feel the motion of a deck under me, and the excitement of arriving in port.

By looking at the journal kept by Ned of the births of the children I see that it was 1799, a full six years since the deaths of our shipmates, and nearly ten years since we came to Pitcairn, when the final bouts of violence brought an end to McCoy and Quintal. Two more babies were born to Ned by his two wives, Prudence gave me Hannah, and Teio bore Catherine to McCoy.

Little Catherine was spared the terror of her father, because McCoy, by the time of her birth, had become a lunatic through drink. All the supplies of intoxicating liquor from the 'Bounty' were long since consumed, leaving only the drink made from the yava root, which the natives found on Pitcairn. The traditional method from Otaheite requires it to be chewed and spat into a bowl where it is infused with leaves, but McCoy, who had once worked at a distillery in Scotland, had been trying other methods and roots. He found the root of a plant called 'Ti', which grows wild everywhere, and ground it up, mixed it with water and made a fermentation. Then he used a large kettle, which Quintal had taken from the 'Bounty', to distil the brew. This gave him a fiery spirit, a sort of arak, which pleased us all more than the yava, and I confess that I liked it well enough.

McCoy then set himself to produce much greater quantities, but then drank so much of it that after a few months it turned his brain. From rising in the morning until he collapsed in a stupor late in the day he became a slave to his creation, and like old Huggan, it killed him, though his passing was more of a spectacle than that drunken old fool of a surgeon. It was already dark one evening, and we were gathered at supper except for McCoy, whom we could hear singing and shouting down the hill from the village. Teio, cradling her baby, was shaking her head in despair.

"Come, Alex, maybe we should go and find him," said Ned.

We took a brand from the fire and walked down the hill to where McCoy was sitting at the cliff-edge, binding a cord round his ankles.

"Will, what on earth are you doing?" cried Ned.

"Ah'm for the gallows," laughed McCoy, "Mr Christian says we're all to hang."

"What nonsense, Mr Christian is not here," I said.

"Aye he is, I can see him there beside you."

As we started towards him, he attempted to rise to his feet, lurched sideways, and fell over the cliff.

We looked for the body the next morning, but found nothing. The surf must have claimed it. Teio came to me weeping, but I think those were tears more of relief than of grief. She had sought the comfort of my arms before, and after that she stayed with me.

McCoy's potion, however, had not finished its evil work, for Quintal became as much addicted. His rages became more violent and even on the rare occasions when he was sober he was not to be reasoned with. Sarah could bear him no more, and ran away. He was too drunk to pursue her, but he turned his rage on other women, and forced himself on Susan, so that after he was dead she bore him a son, Edward.

The end came one evening, when he could be heard, in a drunken rage, bursting into some of the houses in search of a woman on whom he could vent his spleen or his lust. However, the women had all sought sanctuary with Ned and me in our houses, so there were none to be found elsewhere. Then I heard Ned shouting, and looked out to see them grappling at his door. I seized an axe, the only weapon that came to hand, and ran over. Quintal had his hands round Ned's throat. I swung the flat of the axe at his side. He grunted, but did not let go, and I could see that Ned was choking badly, so I raised the axe and clove Matt Quintal's skull, felling him like an ox.

Ned and I sank to the ground, he coughing and gasping for breath, I sobbing and trembling from emotions which I struggled to control. Soft murmurs from the women in the houses rose to cries of relief, joy even, as they emerged from the houses and saw that their tormentor was no more. They brought us cool water to drink, and bathed us, and fanned us, and then brought chairs before Ned's front door, so that we sat enthroned as princes while they sat on the ground around us, singing softly. I felt like no prince, however.

"Dear God, will all my life be thus, Ned? Can I never be free from such strife?"

"Why do you say so, Alex?"

"All my life I have been followed by evil and murder, and they follow me still. I fear God has cursed me."

"There was no avoiding Quintal's fate. He nearly killed me, and if he had done he would have done away with you sooner or later. And, Alex, I have never thought of you as a bad man. How can you say evil pursues you?"

"Ned, I am not Alexander Smith, my real name is John Adams."

And then I unburdened my soul to him, as I believe the Catholicks confess to their priests, although I never saw that. I told him of my childhood as a thief, of the man who was killed when he chased me, of the caretaker whom I murdered, of Redepath's murder, all of it. I said I was ashamed of my part in casting away Bligh and eighteen others to almost certain death, ashamed of invading Tubuai, ashamed of the killings which had turned this island from a refuge to a charnel-house.

"Our prayerbook says 'We have done those things which we ought not to have done, and there is no health in us'. There is no health in me, only despair, and I begin to hate this place."

"But Alex, or rather, John, the prayer continues ' - but though, O Lord, have mercy upon us miserable offenders. Spare thou them O God, which confess their faults. Restore thou them that be penitent.' Now, I am no pastor and can not forgive you your sins, but you can be sure that God has heard what you confessed to me, and if your heart is truly repentant, as I am sure it is, God will forgive you. I know you are not an evil man, such as that Redepath you spoke of, or this poor wretch" - he gestured at Quintal's body lying nearby - "who let the Devil take over his soul. Do not despair! Consider what happened to Christian. He let despair drive him to turn on Bligh, but if he had found some other way of dealing with him than sending them all to their deaths, I am sure we would have followed him, so he must bear the shame of that. And his joy at finding this place turned to misery because he found exile did not suit him. We must not become like him, or ruin ourselves like McCoy and Quintal."

"But how shall we stop this evil?"

"By doing good! We have no reason to kill each other, let us grow old together in peace and tranquility. I do not think the women want to kill us, though they once did, so let us look after them, till our fields, tend our nets and thank God that we have been spared to live a simple life in this pleasant place. But the greatest good we can do is to teach all these children to live in harmony together, without greed and anger. Then surely God will forgive the reckless lives we have lived until now. We must attend to their schooling."

"The only learning I have is what little you have taught me of reading."

"You can help them to learn while you learn more yourself. And you have more to pass on, such as your skills as a fisherman – but most important is the example we set them. If they see us in harmony with each other, and dealing kindly with their mothers, they will grow up to be the same."

"God bless you, Ned, you have given me some hope. Good night."

"Good night, John Adams."

In the morning Quintal's body was gone. I do not know what the women did with it, and I never asked them.

Peace did come to Pitcairn, as Ned foretold. We set to work at our daily tasks, and were joined happily by the women, who now felt themselves secure and free from oppression. Much of the clothing that we had from the 'Bounty' was gone, but their skill at making cloth from tree-bark ensured that we did not go naked. The boats from the 'Bounty', too, were no more, their timbers sprained and rotted, but we made canoes after the style of Otaheite, which were easier to launch through the surf.

There were sixteen children aged three or more at that time, and the oldest, Thursday October, was nearly nine years old. Ned devised some simple reading lessons for them, also exercises in arithmetick, and their mothers sometimes joined the classes. Every morning and evening he read from the prayerbook we had from the 'Bounty', and we observed Sundays with a service of prayers and a reading from the Bible. I became very familiar with the words of those prayers and could recite them from memory. Every day Ned gave me an exercise in reading from the Bible so that my understanding of the written words increased greatly although I could still write little. We also taught the children to give thanks to the Lord before and after every meal.

Thus by a simple and God-fearing life, ways which we still follow today, did we seek to wash away the sins of those former years. So why did God punish us again? Ned became afflicted with some ailment which irritated his lungs, and his breathing became laboured; he said it was asthma, which he had before sometimes when he was a boy but had ceased and he had not expected to be troubled by it again. It became worse, and though

Nancy and Mainmast gave him various potions and bathed him constantly, nothing could ease his distress. I sat by his bed and wept as the final crisis came upon him, as he groaned and gasped until his eyes turned up in his head, toward Heaven, his body gave up the struggle, and his spirit left him.

My dear friend, the best I think I had in my whole life, why did God take him? If we still had to be punished, why did he not take me? I never felt such grief as I did then, and even now I shed a tear when I recall his distress in that final hour.

The grief turned to despair, worse than what oppressed me before, and I thought of ending my life, by throwing myself off a cliff or plunging into the surf to let the sea take me. Dear Teio and the other women tried to console me, but I shied away from their company, and from the children, and the island became a prison to me. I thought I might escape my oppression by working, but after an hour in the field I cast down my hoe, there seemed little purpose in it, and I wept again.

There remained some flagons of McCoy's liquor, which Ned and I had never wanted, but had not troubled to destroy. I found them and sought relief in oblivion. I remember little of the afternoon when I sprawled under a tree drinking steadily from a bottle until I became unconscious. I do not know how long I lay there, but sleep brought me no comfort, for my dreams were troubled and violent. Though I remembered little when I awoke, I had the feeling that I had been haunted by demons, and visited by Woodlea, and Redepath, and the old man I murdered, and Bligh in the boat, and many other accusing ghosts. If, as the Bible tells us, the spirit lives on after the body dies, how could I escape such dreams by taking my own life? This surely was Hell, and God had shown me the punishment that awaited me.

My sweet little Dinah came to me with a cup of water, set it down beside me, and threw her arms round my neck.

"Oh Father," she said, "we were so frightened, you were calling out and crying, and we thought you would die. We could not bear it if you were taken from us."

Then I knew that by the pure innocence of my child, God was showing me the way to salvation. "Do not despair, stop the evil by doing good", Ned had said, and we had set out together on that road. Now I must walk on alone, and though I was but a common sailor with no education and barely able to read, I must show Dinah and all the other children, and their mothers too, the way to a life of peace and harmony, by heeding God's word. Dinah fetched me my Bible, that was really Captain Bligh's, and it fell open at St Matthew's Gospel, where Christ preached to his disciples on the mountain;

"Blessed are the poor in spirit; for theirs is the kingdom of heaven – Blessed are they that mourn; for they shall be comforted – Let your light shine before men, that they may see your good works, and glorify your father which is in heaven."

Jesus was calling me to be His disciple. His words already comforted me in my mourning for Ned. I must be the light for all the souls cast away in this lonely place, and lead them to live a better life than ever I had done before. The pain in my head was still terrible, and my limbs overcome by lassitude, but my heart was easy because I knew that my life still had a purpose.

Chapter 17 – Discovered at last!

I poured away what remained of McCoy's poison, for I had no wish to encounter again the demons that had haunted my sleep, nor did I want the children to have such an example of drunken behaviour, or, God forbid, to sample such evil themselves. Daily, except on the Sabbath, I sat with them all and gave then such lessons as I was able. Ned had left a text of simple words, which I continued, and then I turned to the Bible, where there are many stories, which we read together until they were as familiar with the words of those pages as I. Together we read of Adam and Eve in the garden, while I thought that God had given us such a garden, and I must protect their innocence lest they be cast out into the world of wickedness that I had endured at their age. We read of Moses, who came down from the mountain with God's commandments, which we must keep. We read of Solomon, of David and Goliath, of Daniel in the lion's den, and Jonah in the belly of the whale, which was their favourite, as we often saw the spouts of whales in the sea around us, and they fancied there might be a man in the belly of one of them.

I had to chastise them sometimes for disobedience, and their attention would stray, but I was at first a poor teacher and did not understand that small children will not remain attentive too long at any one task, so must be given other subjects to interest them. Ned had left some pages of simple arithmetick, which I made sure they knew, but could not add anything, as my knowledge was no greater than theirs. I taught them what little I knew of the world, of England and King George, who must be our King also, of Ireland where my father came from but I had never seen, and of the places where the 'Bounty' had called. I told them of London, of the ships I had seen from many countries, and the ships that went to a country called India and came back laden with all manner of things. I told them about the coal which is burned in cold countries like England, how it is dug out of the ground and shipped from Newcastle to London. I told them about money and showed them coins which I had kept, explaining how fortunate they were that we did not need money here, because the pursuit and lust for money were the cause of much violence and misery, and the lack of it too. I did not tell them of my own misdeeds in pursuit of it.

Sometimes they asked about their fathers, and I said they were all good men who had sought a better life on this island, but we were so weakened by severity of the voyage in coming here that only I survived the illnesses which had overtaken us, and they were now in Heaven. I think their mothers also wanted to protect their innocence and gave no contrary account. The children all spoke English, though with some Otaheitean words that they learned from their mothers. The women mostly came to Sunday prayers with their children, though they had then but a small understanding of our worship.

The years passed, and I daily thanked God, as I still do, for the settled and peaceful life which he granted to us. Four years after Ned's death Teio gave me a son, whom I named George after our King. When that boy was nearly four years old, there came the event about which I used to worry when we first came to Pitcairn, but had long since faded from my thoughts – a ship was spied approaching from the east, it drew nearer and dropped anchor in Bounty Bay.

Finally we were discovered, and I wondered whether this might be the end of my peaceful life. Should I run with a musket to Christian's cave, and sell my life dearly, as he had sworn to do? The ship did not look like a Navy ship. I could not discern the flag she flew, but it did not look like the Ensign. Maybe they had just come for wood and water, which they could take and leave without any dealings with us. However, I saw that Thursday October, now a fine youth, with two others had launched through the surf, and their canoe was speeding towards the ship. There could be no question of avoiding contact now, and there seemed little purpose in fleeing. The island is not so big, and they could find me eventually if they wished. There would be no muskets, I could not now return to my murdering ways. I saw the canoe start back, with the three boys accompanied by one other. I retired to my house to await my fate.

A while later Thursday October came in to me.

"I have brought Captain Folger of the Topaz. He is English."

"You foolish boy," hissed Teio, "why did you bring him to us? Do not go out, husband, we can give him what he wants and send him away."

"Nay, sooner or later this must be faced," I replied, and went out to greet the stranger.

"Captain Mayhew Folger, of the whaler 'Topaz', out of Boston, at your service."

"Boston, on the Wash? The boy said you are English."

"Nay, Boston Massachusetts, of the United States of America. I beg your pardon, I told him English because I thought he would understand that better."

"America, is that near Ireland?" asked Thursday October.

"Nay, it is thousands of miles to the west of Ireland," laughed the Captain, "though there are a fair few Irish people in Boston."

When I was in trouble as a boy before the Blind Beak, all I knew of America was that Virginia was a colony where convicts might be sent, or you might be kidnapped from any street in England and sold as a slave on the plantations, but I heard afterwards that those colonies fought a war against England and became an independent country with no allegiance to King George. Captain Folger sounded a little like Isaac Martin, and I knew I was safe because he was American.

"My name is John Adams, sir," I said.

"The boy says his father sailed with Captain Bligh. I did read in the newspaper about the 'Bounty' – so is this where she came?"

"Indeed, sir, and I sailed on her also, but my name on the ship was Alexander Smith."

"And this island is Pitcairn?"

"Aye, sir, the chart gives an incorrect position, where there is no island. But may I ask, what was written about us in the newspaper?"

"Well, I remember little of the detail, except the ship was taken by an officer named Christian - "

"That was my father!" exclaimed Thursday October.

"- aye, and Captain Bligh and his men made a heroic voyage of four thousand miles to the Dutch East Indies, and all but one arrived there."

"Captain Bligh lives?" I cried.

"He did then, and when he came back to England he was much celebrated."

"And what of the mutineers who stayed on Otaheite?"

"Oh, I know nothing of that, I do not see a newspaper very often."

I was overcome with a strange joy that Captain Bligh had not perished because of our cruelty, even though I have no doubt that had he stood before me then, he would not have hesitated to have me arrested and sent to the gallows.

Captain Folger and some of his crew were made welcome with a feast, and I told him a little of our history, although I did not feel it necessary to give an account as detailed as this of events before the mutiny, or of my part in it. I told him I was asleep when the ship was taken, and had just gone along with the rest. We sailed to Otaheite and left some of the mutineers there, then we found Pitcairn. Of our early years here, I said the strife between us and the native men had led to them killing all but me, and the women in turn had killed those men.

There was a Second Mate who made advances to Elizabeth Mills, and that angered me greatly. The impudent fellow then tried to engage me further about the fate of Mr Christian and the others. I told him that Christian had become insane soon after we came to Pitcairn and had thrown himself off a cliff, but I would not trouble with further explanation to such an ill-mannered person.

I was pleased, however, to have the company after so many years of a gentleman such as Captain Folger. He told me that England was now at war with France, and a great Admiral, Lord Nelson, had won a sea-battle at a place called Trafalgar, which gave England mastery of the seas.

"Old England for ever!" I cried.

I gave him remembrances of the 'Bounty', its chronometer and a compass. He gave me a silk handkerchief, which I still treasure. It was the only one I had since I stole them from the pockets of gentlemen and ladies in London some forty years before.

As Captain Folger arose to take his leave, my little daughter Hannah came up to him.

"If you please, sir, do you catch whales from your ship?"

"Indeed we do, and seals."

"And have you ever found a man in the belly of a whale?"

"Why, no," the Captain roared with laughter, "it must have been a very special whale that swallowed Jonah, and there are none like that in this ocean!"

Chapter 18 – Rediscovered

Before he left, Captain Folger asked me if I would object to him making a report to the newspapers of his discovery and visit. In a vainglorious moment I said I did not, for I doubted the Navy could ever find me here. It may have been foolish, but in truth even if I had objected, it would be expecting much of anyone to forbear mentioning such an unusual story as ours for long. In any case, nothing could prevent the tongues of such rogues as that Second Mate from wagging.

Thus our lives continued as before, except I daily cast an eye seawards for the next ship that must surely arrive before long. Thursday October grew to manhood, followed by Matthew Quintal, Charles Christian, and those others who had come into our little world when it was still in great turmoil. What a triumph for God's Word it is, that young Matthew is as honest and kindly a man as his father was a vicious uncaring rascal! And it is a great joy to see that these young men and women always observed a chaste propriety, nor was there ever any lewd behaviour by any of them, even though the women go about in the style of Otaheite and are often unclothed above the waist, which was always a great temptation when I was a young sailor. All the young people, and their mothers, looked to me for guidance, there were few disputes, and we shared all we had. And still no ship came, though I sometimes espied one many leagues distant.

Then, a full six years after Captain Folger's visit, I saw two ships come from the north. For hours I watched their approach, and as they anchored I felt that little stab of fear and my heart beat faster. These were no fishing-boats, they were warships, far bigger than the 'Bounty', with up to twenty gun-ports along each side, and they flew the Ensign of His Majesty's Ships. The Navy had come for me at last, after twenty-five years. Dear God, was I such a villain that they had to send two ships? Was my sentence already passed, was I to be hanged from a yard-arm out there in the bay, or would they take me back to London? I thought I would prefer the former, so that my last sight would be of Pitcairn, my home, but that would be terrible for my family to see; my mind was confused and I knew not what to do.

As before, I saw Thursday October and Edward Young, Ned's son, paddling towards the ships in their canoe. They climbed aboard and after some minutes disappeared below, where they remained for some time. Finally they emerged, and with two passengers made for the shore.

"There come but two of them," I said to Teio, to whom I was describing everything as her eyesight had become very poor.

"Good. If only two, I think they not take you," she replied.

We went out to greet our visitors, who wore officers' uniforms like Bligh's which were quite wet from their journey through the surf. One of them had only one arm.

"Welcome to Pitcairn. I am John Adams."

"Captains Sir Thomas Staines and Philip Pipon of His Majesty's Ships 'Briton' and 'Tagus'" said the one-armed one. "So this is Pitcairn, you say? There is no island marked on the chart, which is why we came to survey it. Then we saw your settlement, and your young men have told us an extraordinary story of the 'Bounty'."

"So you did not have news of us from Captain Folger, sir?"

"Who is Captain Folger? No, we have heard nothing."

My mind eased as I realised that they knew nothing of us, and had not been sent for me, although I supposed they could still decide to take me. We sat down together, and the women brought us refreshments. I noticed that Captain Pipon was taken aback when he saw my Hannah, who had not troubled to cover her bosom, as she and most of the women rarely did, but he was a gentleman and did not stare or pass comment. I told them of how we had come here after taking the 'Bounty', and of the discord we had in those early years which had left me the sole survivor. Of the mutiny I said I had known little when it happened, because I was sick in bed. I told them I was enlisted on the 'Bounty' as Alexander Smith.

"How so?" asked Captain Staines.

"I was much pursued by the bailiffs, sir, and had only a life in a debtor's prison to look forward to. But, sir, did you truly have no knowledge of us?"

"Not at all, Adams, our orders contain nothing about Pitcairn or you."

"And may I enquire, sir, about Captain Bligh? Captain Folger said that he survived from the boat, and his voyage was much celebrated in England."

"Indeed it was. If I remember correctly, he was given another ship and was commended by Nelson for his action at the Battle of Copenhagen. I believe he was more recently promoted to Vice Admiral."

"Some who mutinied preferred to stay on Otaheite. Did you hear of them, sir?"

"Indeed, they were found and taken on a ship – I forget the name -"

"The Pandora, under Captain Edwards," said Captain Pipon.

"Quite so. But the ship foundered on a reef off Australia and some of the mutineers were drowned."

"I never heard of Australia," I said.

"That is what we now call New Holland, and it will become a great part of His Majesty's dominions. However, the remaining mutineers faced a court-martial where some were acquitted, but six were found guilty and sentenced to death."

"I believe two received His Majesty's pardon," said Captain Pipon, "one of them was Heywood, who came back in the Navy and is already made Post Captain."

So Mr Christian had always been right, that the Navy would go back to Otaheite and take anyone who stayed there. And that little weasel Peter Heywood had saved his neck after all. But would I save mine?

The Captains took great interest in our houses, our plantations and asked many questions about our life here. Finally Captain Staines said,

"I must say, Adams, this is remarkable. You seem to have created an English village on the other side of the world from England."

"Thank you, sir. I have only done my best to bring these people to fear God and be loyal subjects of King George."

"That is fine. I fear the old King is become unwell, and we are now governed by the Prince Regent, but all will be well when we have finally beaten Napoleon – ah yes, you will not have heard of him, an upstart Frenchman who sought to conquer all of Europe, but we will take him down at last."

"I heard something of a war with the French from Captain Folger."

"He was American, was he not? Beware of them, they are not to be trusted. But tell me, Adams, have you never wished to see England again?"

This was a longing that had come to me sometimes, though it is hard to fathom why, because my life here was easier than ever it had been there. Perhaps I lacked the company of other men like myself, and I certainly wondered whether my brother lived, and how he fared. Captain Staines was not taking me prisoner, so maybe I would be safe in England.

"I think I might like to go there," I replied.

However, when word that I might go passed around the village, nearly all assembled around us, and Hannah dropped to her knees before Captain Staines and cried,

"Oh, do not, sir, take from me my father, do not take away my best, my dearest friend!"

Her weeping brought forth tears and cries from many others, and the Captains were overwhelmed by the display of affection and loyalty, as I was also.

"Very well, Mr Adams, it is clearly your right and your duty to remain here. I am sure that the good that you have wrought in this little colony will be well received by all in England, even by His Highness the Prince Regent himself."

Now I was no longer 'Adams', a common seaman and mutineer, I was 'Mr Adams', the Father of a colony.

Chapter 19 – The world comes to Pitcairn

As Captains Staines and Pipon were ferried back to their ships, I experienced a great wave of relief and satisfaction, not just that I now had little reason to believe I would ever be carried away and tried for my life, but that I was no longer an outcast, and our little island would be known about and spoken of in the rest of the world.

I do not know how long it took the news to reach England, and it was certainly many months, maybe more than a year before we saw another ship, but then we saw a few each year, many bearing messages of goodwill, and gifts; one was a book, I have it still, inscribed by Sir William Sydney Smith, who had been commander of the Navy in South America and had seen Captain Folger's report of his discovery. It is a very fine volume, entitled 'Robinson Crusoe', about a man cast away on a Pacific island. I dare say Sir William thought I might find it instructive, but in truth it was difficult to read.

We welcome all the visitors when they come, and are at pains to display to them what they expect to see, the good order of our community, of our houses and plantations, our piety and observance of the Sabbath. In truth we have nothing else to show them, for that is how we live, but I sometimes think that we are in a circus, or have been made the subject of a zoology. How many times have I recounted the story of how we came here, and those early dark years on which I prefer not to dwell. I became weary of the telling of it, and have not always said the same things. It is strange that I am never asked about my early years, or how I came to be on the 'Bounty', for which I am thankful. Instead they all want to talk about Mr Christian, for it seems there are now many legends attached to him. Indeed, one lady who came thought I was Mr Christian, for she had seen a play in London about it, and would not be disabused of the notion for some time. However, I am happy to see all these visitors because they do not come so often, and I would not like to be cut off from the rest of the world as we were for so many years.

Of the visits we have had, I recall another whaler, the 'Sultan', which happened upon us by accident, as Captain Folger had done, and did not know of our existence. Captain Reynolds was a most amiable man, and invited me to dine on his ship, the first time I had been aboard a sea-going vessel since the 'Bounty'. I made a show of climbing the rigging and singing a shanty, which amused all of the crew, who were most hospitable. I do not know why Captain Staines said Americans were not to be trusted, as lately they were our own kith and kin, but I have little understanding of the politics and the wars that were fought then.

It was the 'Sultan' in which Jenny went away. I do not think she hated Pitcairn so much, but she had not wanted to leave Otaheite, and when Captain Reynolds said he hoped to pass that way she decided to go with him. I hope she found her own people, and is happy.

The kindness of the people of England was evident from the gifts, we received, clothing, tools, fishing hooks, blankets, and much more, as well as texts to aid our worship, some of which I have read. But the greatest joy of all has been to receive correspondence from my brother. His first letter was dated some time in 1818, and he said he had been filled with joy when he read about me in a newspaper. He was sound in health and substance, and had good employment as a fireman with an assurance company in London. He hoped he might see me in England, if that were ever possible. I replied, with the assistance of the clerk on one of the ships, that I did not expect it would be possible. So, my little brother had succeeded in growing up from the Hackney poorhouse to an honest life in London, which I failed to do, but I hope I have made amends for that.

Another important visit came six years ago, in 1823, which is easily remembered because John Buffet, who is writing this for me, arrived on a whaler named the 'Cyrus'. Mr Buffet is an Englishman, from Bristol, skilled as a carpenter and shipwright, and had such a great impression of our community that he expressed a desire to stay here with us. We talked awhile, and I could see that he is an honest and God-fearing man, but what is more, his education is superior to mine, so that he has been able to take over the teaching of our young people and to assist with our prayers. I was very happy to have him join us and share my burden, and he was granted permission by his Captain to leave the ship. I did not expect that he would be accompanied by another, John Evans, a young man from London, who contrived to come ashore without permission and remained when the ship sailed.

These, then were the first to choose Pitcairn as their home since those of us who arrived on the 'Bounty'. Mr Buffet is now married to Dorothy, one of Ned's daughters, and young Evans has married my Rachel. The children of my dead shipmates are all grown up, and many have married. I always counsel them not to marry too young till they have acquired sufficient property to bring up a young family, and none have married without my blessing. Now there will be another generation to carry on life here, and to serve God and the King.

Four years ago there came HMS 'Blossom', under Captain Beechey, and remained above two weeks. As it approached, we manned our canoe, I with a number of our young men, and sailed out a great way to meet it. I went aboard and was greeted by Captain Beechey and his Officers, and was quickly led to his cabin, where he was eager, as many had been before, to hear the story of how we came to Pitcairn. I could only tell him what is more or less recorded in these pages, and he had a clerk there taking a record. It crossed my mind that this might be intended as the basis of an indictment, but Captain Beechey gave no sign of that, and was exceedingly friendly. We spent a long time below, and John Buffet told me that those watching from the shore were greatly afraid that I had been taken, and were much relieved when I came back on deck and got into our boat.

On another day I went aboard the 'Blossom' again, to be entertained by Officers in the Gun Room. On that occasion I fear that I lapsed from my normal sobriety because the familiar sights and sounds of a Navy ship gave me a longing to taste the grog once again, and though I think I drank but little, it had a great effect on me, as I was no longer accustomed to it. There was one Officer, Lieutenant Belcher, who asked me many questions about the 'Bounty' and the mutiny, which I answered as best I could remember with the drink inside me. Oh, how many versions of the 'Bounty' story must there be now, how many interpretations of my words?

The crew of the 'Blossom' spent much time ashore with us, and shared in our prayers, our meal-times, and showed interest in the traditions that were born in Otaheite. On one evening they requested a heiva to be danced by the women, but only three would do so, and only for a minute or two, because such a display is not commensurate with our customs on Pitcairn. However, I took the opportunity to ask Captain Beechey to read the marriage service over Teio and myself, which he was pleased to do, so now we are married before God under English Law.

Lionel Pettrick

Chapter 20 – Paradise?

Of those who came to Pitcairn nearly forty years ago there remain but five of the women and myself. However, now two generations have followed and we number above sixty. I have wondered often in recent times what shall be done if our numbers rise much more, and can not be sustained by the island. If we take too much out of the soil, if we fell all the timber, we will not so easily feed and provide shelter for ourselves as we always have done. I also worry that our supply of water may fail one day, as we rely on rainfall to maintain the few streams that we have, and in the drier months we have barely enough as it is. I have passed on such concerns to Captain Beechey and others who have come, and hope that the Government in London will consider what should be done to save our little colony, which was always loyal to His Majesty. If it can not be sustained here, maybe they would grant us land in New Holland, or Australia as it is called. But we must be placed where we may continue our Godly way of life without interference. Above all, our children should be protected from the evils of the world, as I think I never was.

It is, however, for another to take up the burden that I carried these many years. I am happy that with God's guidance my yoke has been easy, my burden light, and my heart swells with pride and love when they call me 'Father'. But soon I, too, must pay the debt of nature, and my people will need someone else to lead them. I have told them they should convene and elect one of them to succeed me, which they have not done, I think because they prefer to wait until I go.

I would be happy for John Buffet to carry on my work, because he wrought much improvement in the education of our children, and in our worship, for he delivers better sermons than I could. He is also, like his young friend John Evans, honest and hard-working, and can do much to improve the building of our houses and much else. However, there has come in this last year a man called George Nobbs. He has the trappings of an educated gentleman, and quickly persuaded many families that he could give their children a better education than they received from Mr Buffet, so that they all attended his lessons, and Mr Buffet no longer teaches. Mr Nobbs sought to impress me by claiming that he is the illegitimate son of the Marquis of Hastings, but spoke no more of it after I told him that being anyone's bastard could not commend him to me or to any God-fearing person on Pitcairn. He gives himself the airs of a preacher also, though he has not yet dared to try and take my place. I fear that his manner of superiority does not sit well with the practices of our community. If he assumes leadership when I have gone, he will have a hard time of it without the goodwill of all, but he must learn that for himself, else he may spend many of his days in the cave of the last gentleman who came to live on Pitcairn. But these days I have little strength to argue over such matters.

There is little more I wish to say or remember about my life. I might have ended my young days on the gallows, and it is strange that I was able to come here and live a peaceful and honest life only by the mutiny, which should also have brought me to the gallows. So from an evil act I hope some good has come. But then, if I had not mutinied, and gone with Captain Bligh, could I not have lived an honest life back in England, though I hardly did before? It seems that my brother does well there, so could not I also? Or is it only by being in a place like this, freed from the temptations of society, that I can avoid sin? Is the faith that I have found here strong enough to keep me on the path of righteousness in a world of wickedness elsewhere?

People spoke of Otaheite as Paradise, but it was not. Though provided with all the bounty of nature, a warm sun, pure air and water, and a freedom from want, yet people had the failings to be found in all mankind. They did not scruple to steal if they though there was no punishment, and though there was peace while we were there, I heard that there had often been disputes or wars between tribes, and between islands, so Tynah had to defend himself against others, as King George must against France. And, however placid their disposition, and displaying the innocence of children in their dealings with us and each other, I cannot understand how such people could also regard it as a normal custom to kill their babies. It is a terrible thing to take a life, and I know the feeling of dread and sickness that comes on one who has killed. Did they feel nothing of that?

I have also heard visitors here exclaim that Pitcairn is Paradise, but it seemed not so to Mr Christian or any of us who were caught up in the strife and murder of those early years. I truly think there is no earthly Paradise, and those who seek such a thing do not understand the nature of man, or God's will. But Hell can befall us as easily in this life as in the next, because the Devil lurks in men's souls, and the sinner is in Hell already, though he knows it not, and his weakness may also create a Hell on Earth for other people. My whole life was worthless until I heeded the Word of God, and I pray that those who call me 'Father', and all who come after them, will have the strength to keep Pitcairn safe from the wickedness of the world and the wiles of the Devil.

But let me rest now. The unceasing sound of the surf brings balm to my soul, and if it follows me beyond the grave, I will know that God has forgiven me my sins.

Epilogue

The testament in these pages was made to me over many afternoons by John Adams, and I transcribed it later. If I have not always given his exact words, I trust that I have faithfully rendered his meaning.

John Adams went to his Eternal Rest on the Fifth Day of this Month, and his wife Teio followed him nine days later. May Almighty God bestow His blessings on one who repented his sins and sought the salvation of a righteous life for himself and all who loved him, and called him 'Father'.

J. Buffet   30th March 1829

Author's Note

I am no historian, and the reader should not regard this tale as historical fact, if there is such a thing. In the early Nineteenth Century, after the settlement on Pitcairn had become known to the outside world, Sir John Barrow, Permanent Secretary to the Admiralty, presented the 'Bounty' story, and John Adams's part in establishing Pitcairn, as a sort of morality tale, a triumph of good over evil. Victorian England and sundry religious societies of the time eagerly bought into this version. It's not an unreasonable take on all those events, and I found it interesting.

Apart from the Hackney Parish records which confirm the birth of John Adams (baptised December 4 1767) and those of his siblings, almost nothing is known about him before he joined the 'Bounty'. He scrawled a few lines on Pitcairn stating that his father was drowned in the Thames and left him an orphan, and that's all. So, it is important to emphasise that there is absolutely no evidence that he was a thief and a murderer in his early years. However, he must have had a reason for enlisting on the 'Bounty' as Alexander Smith, which gives licence for speculation, and one piece of research into his antecedents stated that he also used the alias Alexander Gow, so I included that in my tale as well.

Contemporary accounts of the 'Bounty's voyage, and subsequent events, serve to illustrate that witnesses to the same event may differ significantly in their versions of what happened. Bligh himself in his Journal gives little indication of any discord sufficient to justify his being turfed out of bed one morning and booted off his ship. James Morrison, the Boatswain's Mate, wrote an articulate and damning account of Bligh's captaincy, strongly motivated no doubt by his desire to escape being hanged (and he was pardoned by the King). Barrow's 'History' included a hagiography of Peter Heywood, the young Midshipman, whose family connections played a large part in his being granted a Royal Pardon, and they also contributed to the campaign to denigrate Bligh. Witness statements at the court-martial do not give a consistent picture of who did what, and when. Fletcher Christian's family also launched their own 'enquiry' and publicity campaign against Bligh to mitigate the shame that mutineer had brought on them.

To cap it all, Adams gave differing accounts of his part in the mutiny and of the demise of his comrades on Pitcairn, as I tried to show in this tale. I have selected, from various sources, a version of the voyage of the 'Bounty' and everything that happened thereafter, as it might have appeared to a common uneducated seaman. I hope that any 'colour' I have added does not offend anyone's perception of the "facts" too much, and if it seems too unlikely that Adams's amanuensis, John Buffet, more artisan than scholar, would have been capable of such prose, I claim artistic licence. The most comprehensive account of this extraordinary episode in history, encompassing truth, half-truth, supposition and myth, may be found in 'The Bounty' by Caroline Alexander, a fascinating and very readable work of great scholarship. Myths abounded; Barrow records that Fletcher Christian was allegedly seen in England in 1808. So much for history.

None of it would have happened if Sir Joseph Banks, President of the Royal Society, had not hit on the notion of transplanting the Breadfruit from the Pacific to the Caribbean. An acquaintance of mine in Thailand has a Breadfruit in his garden, a fine large tree with huge beautiful leaves. He gave me some fruits which I attempted to bake as described in Bligh's Journal (and originally in Captain Cook's). I am sorry to report that I did not manage the result given by Bligh - "..the inside is soft, tender and white like the crumb of a penny loaf." James Morrison wrote that "its colour inside when baked is yellowish and its consistency like that of a potato", which is nearer to what I achieved. I can't say it was particularly appetising.

The 'Ti' plant (Dracaena terminalis), from whose roots McCoy brewed and distilled the spirit which killed him, is quite common hereabouts, and there are variants in our garden. Being keen to preserve my eyesight and my sanity, I have not been tempted to reproduce McCoy's vodka.

If my tale does not portray William Bligh in a sympathetic light, I would like to place on record that, whatever his alleged failings, his 4000 mile voyage in an open boat with eighteen men, only one of whom was killed en route, was a feat of seamanship, navigation and leadership without parallel. I salute his memory, and that of John Adams, Pitcairn's Father.

Lionel Pettrick   March 2019

About the Author

Lionel Pettrick is British, was born in North Wales in 1944, grew up mainly in Sheffield, and also worked for an engineering company in that city for twenty-two years. He later moved to the south of England, spending twenty years in the Immigration Service. Since retirement he has lived in Thailand. Many years of sailing on the English Channel and elsewhere have instilled in him an unbounded admiration for the men (and women) of former centuries who took to the world's oceans in wooden sailing ships.

He has one previous work - "Dillflower – the scribblings of an old fart in Thailand" which was published as an e-book in 2018.

Many thanks for reading this book. If you have enjoyed it, please leave a recommendation with the retailer where you purchased it.

Printed in Great Britain
by Amazon